Hyperion

Jack Rambler

Hyperion by Jack Rambler

www.ramblersden.com

© 2017 "Jack Rambler"

All rights reserved. No portion of this book may be reproduced in any form without permission from the publisher, except as permitted by U.S. copyright law.

For permissions contact:

theramblersden@gmail.com

Cover Art by Manthos Lappas

For you.

Without you this wouldn't exist.

Thank you.

And as always, thank you for reading!

Jack

Chapter I

I wake slowly, swinging my legs off the bed and resting my feet on the cold concrete floor. I ease myself up onto tense muscles and stand, stretching my back until a series of satisfying *pops* run up my spine.

Then I lean forward and reach down, letting my calves stretch until they feel loose again. I go through the motions for my arms and shoulders until my body aches disappear and I feel ready to face the next piece of my routine.

I trot out of my small bedroom and begin jogging, as I have every single morning for a very, very long time. The air is stale but that doesn't matter much to me, you have to expect as much this deep underground. This cell is built to contain just one prisoner.

That would be me.

It's fully functional, even still, with energy being drawn from the deep core heat of the earth and everything within the cells was built to last. The architect of the prison had designed it that way. After all, it was expected I'd be captive here for a long time.

Not this long though.

The room I sleep in exits into a larger rectangular chamber, with exercise equipment gathered in the center, as well as a perimeter running track. At one end is the kitchen with a small garden sunk into volcanic earth, bolstered by powers beyond the mortal realm. It provides what little sustenance I require. Food is the hardest thing to deal with now, it's just so boring after all these years.

The other end is a library, stocked at my request. I didn't expect I'd have this long, so everything has been read more than a few times. It's not much better than the food situation.

They did expect me to be here a long time.

Just...not this long.

I finish running, stop and bend over, taking deep breaths to slow my heart rate again, letting the sweat drip onto the floor. As habit will do, I look up to the viewing station where the guards had once kept vigil. The station's emptiness reminds me that no one has monitored me for many, many years.

I shake it off and make my way to the kitchen for breakfast. I'm not permitted fire so raw vegetables it is. Delightful.

What I wouldn't give for...well I don't even know anymore. It's been too long, I honestly don't even remember what food options there used to be.

I sigh, clean the dish and make my way to the small washroom. I shower, the water is cold, but I've come to accept the refreshment it brings. When I step out of the shower, I see myself in the mirror and stop to stare.

I flex in the reflective surface and wonder where I've gone. If I hadn't watched myself change over these years I wouldn't recognize myself.

My hair is streaked with grey, what thin hair I have left. My face is tight, pulled back over bones and spotted with age. Age. I don't age as a mortal might and the hands of time will never be the end of my life, but I can certainly fade.

And fade I have.

Once powerful arms have become thin even with the daily exercises, as have my legs even with the daily running. I chuckle at the man in the mirror.

"Some Titan you are, some god of sun and fire. You look old, Hyperion, gone grey and thin." I would glare at him, but the face is mine and I'm not much for self-hate. Self-pity is acceptable.

"You look terrible," I say to the face that used to be a god and leave the washroom before the pity gets worse.

I make my way to the library. I select a book with a nearly tattered spine and sit in the chair that has become my companion these past years. A good companion indeed.

I settle in and begin reading the book, even though by now I can probably recite it from memory. At least the mortals had been kind enough to provide this much for my imprisonment. If only they had stuck around to let me out on time. I shut the book and sigh, leaning back and staring at the gray ceiling. Somewhere, far above where I sit now, there is sunlight. I close my eyes and imagine it but…I can't remember what it feels like. It's been far too long. I can still feel it though, even this deep. I know my sun is up there.

I replace the book and walk to the center room again to ponder what I could spend my time on. Perhaps more standing around, or maybe it's a pacing sort of day. As I walk I see something move out of the corner of my eye and I look to see figures moving in the viewing station.

I stop. There was no one there just a few moments ago.

It can't be.

Guards? After all these years?

A light comes on and I see them, tiny figures barely visible through the dirty glass. I hear a dull *click*. I used to hear that when the guards wanted to speak to us from the perch. With that, I hear voices coming into the room.

"Who is it?" the voices say, along with other chattering and talking before they realize I can hear them. I suppose the staring up at them gave it away.

"Who are you?"

How kind of them to pose it directly to me now.

"One of the great gods. Has it been so long the mortals have forgotten that?"

More indistinct chatter.

"When were you locked in here?"

Now that is a good question. I think back to the day the mortals created this place for us, many thousands of years now surely. I do some quick math before answering.

"Three thousand, one hundred and forty cycles. Around the sun, of course. Perhaps more. Perhaps less."

The murmuring again.

"Impossible," is the reply.

I laugh.

"No, just inconvenient. I was meant to be released after one thousand cycles, but something happened. The guards disappeared."

Murmuring. Goodness these mortals do love to talk, don't they?

"Perhaps you can release me? I'll be eternally grateful."

I chuckle at my own joke. One must become one's own entertainment I suppose. They don't speak for a long time. So long I begin to think they won't help me. I can't even hear the murmuring.

"I'm afraid we can't."

"Please," I say, hearing the begging tone slip into my voice, "please, it's been a very long time."

"I'm sorry."

click

I am ashamed to admit that I dropped to the floor and started weeping.

After recovering from my shameful display of emotion, I find myself sitting in the library but unable to focus. There were mortals alive out there, that was something. Perhaps in a few more cycles they would release me. Surely, just a few more. I would be grateful, and gratitude from some goes a long way.

They have forgotten. They are mortal so that is not so surprising even though we had left them with a bright future. What had gone wrong? Why had they left?

Perhaps more importantly: why had they now come back?

Questions and more questions without any answers. How…irritating.

I sit in the library and ponder these questions until I hear something. Something different. Something I haven't heard in a very, very long time. The main door unlocking. I hear the *hiss* of the door opening and quickly make my way to the main room.

A change of mind? A mortal that does remember?

A young man stands there and looks at me, nervously. He holds up both hands in a sort of mock surrender.

"I just…I don't think it's right to leave you here."

I take a few great strides to him and he flinches. I don't visit violence on him. Not yet. I simply wrap my arms around him and squeeze.

"Thank you," I whisper in his ear, tears filling my eyes. "Thank you."

I was not lying about my gratitude. This man shall have it, forever.

I release him, and we exit the room together, hopefully for the last time. As I take my first step out, I am struck by several barbed objects that sink deep into my flesh, and then I begin to convulse. My muscles tighten, my jaw clamps shut, and I collapse to the floor. A dozen men quickly converge and chain me with the restraints that must have been left in the guard room. Restraints that were designed to contain me.

The barbed objects are new. I don't recall those existing before. I would remember that.

One of them, a burly man with a shaved head, stares down at me.

"*Immortal*, they said," he sneers. "Thousands of years down here? Immortal. Well, we'll see."

The tread of a boot fills my view and is the last thing I see before everything goes dark.

Chapter II

I wake slowly, swinging my legs off the bed and resting my feet on the cold tiled floor. I try to ease myself up onto tense muscles. They don't answer the call as pain shoots through my legs. I remain sitting and stretch my back until a series of *pops* run up my spine. It burns like ice, a reminder of their needles and scalpels and invasive procedures.

I lean forward and reach down, barely reaching my knees before the screaming pain in my calves forces me to stop. I go through the motions for my arms and shoulders, but my body aches don't disappear.

If I had the space to take a run I most certainly would not be able to.

There are scars on my legs from their brutal hands. They tore open my muscles and skin in their efforts to understand what makes me immortal. They stole marrow from my bones, sliced muscles apart to see how they functioned, drew blood and did all of it with detachment bordering on the insane.

Even as I screamed in pain, threatened to burn their world to ash and, when none of that worked, begged for them to cease.

None of that worked.

I remember his laughter as I drifted in and out of consciousness.

"Some god," he said at least once, "some immortal."

I wanted to explain that immortal does not mean invincible. I don't think he would have cared. They wanted to know how to fight aging and disease more than they cared about semantics. Mortals are always seeking what they should not and cannot have, though they seem to have advanced quite a bit from what I remember.

They want the cure to the only disease the mortals are truly plagued by. Death.

I try to stand again but my legs shake and refuse to cooperate again.

I think back to that surgical table they had strapped me to, using those restraints they had found. I think back to the first cuts and the needles drawing blood and the surgeons milling about with their clinical curiosity. I don't blame them. Just the one that suggested they steal from my very bones, him I will kill.

It didn't take long for the pain to become too much to bear and I told them everything.

I am a Titan. Three thousand years ago we started a war, where brother set upon brother and blood flowed as strong as any river. When the bodies were piled high and the mortal realm devastated to the brink of irreparable was when the war ended. When Titans with clear minds stood against those blinded by a lust for war. As punishment we accepted imprisonment, to give the mortals a fighting chance without serving at the whims of gods.

One thousand years, it was to be.

Until the guards stopped coming and the years passed beyond our term. Yet we could not escape our own prison, what would the point have been?

They exchanged strange looks when they learned the facility had been built almost three thousand years ago. I suppose that mortal minds have a hard time comprehending such lengths of time, a blink for an immortal and several lifetimes for others.

I was astounded by how much these mortals had added. The prison had been large for the Titans, it had to be, but now it was staggering in size. The labyrinth of halls and rooms spread out and are filled with armed guards and medical personnel.

And more cells. Like this one.

I am startled by a knock on the door.

"Hey," I hear the voice coming from the door to my new cell, "I'm sorry."

I recognize him. The one who "released" me from my former prison, only to bring me to another.

"You."

"Yeah…I get it," I hear the door unlock from the other side, "I'd be pissed too."

The door opens, and he stands before me, sheepish. Again, his hands are held in mock surrender.

"It wasn't right, I'm sorry. They forced me into it but…I just can't watch them do this to you anymore."

I find the strength to stand on shaky legs and glare at him, but I must admit that he is here, standing before me. Apologetic and releasing me. Hopefully.

A Titan hoping! I'm glad my siblings aren't here to see it.

"Is it day?" I ask him, wrapping an arm over his shoulder and leaning on him heavily.

He nods, with a confused look.

"Can you get me outside?"

He nods again and leads me into the hall, devoid of guards for the moment.

"I opened one of the other cells, they're busy."

"Which one?" I ask, thrilled at the prospect of one of my brothers or sisters on the loose.

"Don't know, names are all faded off the doors. What…who are you anyway?"

I don't speak but we close the gap towards a door, a door that leads to stairs. I glare at him for a moment and he shrugs in response.

"Only way up."

I grunt a sort of agreement and we begin the arduous trek up the stairs. Each one sends pain shooting through my battered legs. I mumble some curses but continue climbing the stairs, lifting my legs despite the pain.

No mortal will see a Titan fail on a simple stairwell. Not today. Not ever.

When the door opens, I feel it. The warmth of the sun. I take a deep breath and almost immediately stand on my own as the warmth and light do their work. The only things I really need. I can feel lean muscles filling out, my hair turning from gray to its proper deep brown and the lines that crease my face disappearing. The ache flees from the warmth like a shadow from light and my body strengthens. I feel…I feel like myself again.

We stand on a flat space with a large white symbol painted on it, overlooking a mountain range that I barely remember. I turn to my rescuer and he sees a new man. He steps back and looks at me with fear. Without the sun I was fading in that deep cell, even if I would have never died of old age there. I looked like a mortal in his fifties or sixties, not the powerful man I am now.

"*What* are you?"

I turn to him and stretch until I hear that satisfying *pop* of my spine. Turn my head for the same in a stiff neck. Bend down to loosen up my calf muscles on healed legs. Open up with a wide stretch to really drink in the power of the light.

"What is your name, mortal?"

"Derek." He stands there, afraid.

"Are you going to kill me?"

I throw my head back and laugh, it feels good to laugh again.

"No, Derek, you have earned my favor. And a favor from me does not come easily. Shall we release my brothers and sisters?"

He swallows hard and nods. Then he asks it again.

"Who...who are you?"

I open the door back to that staircase, down into the bowels of the facility they have built over our prison. It's different now. I have my strength back. That's all the power I need. I pause to look at him, applying just the right amount of dramatic pause that these mortals found so pleasing all those years ago.

Theatrics are important.

"I am the Titan Hyperion. Now come. We have work to do."

We make our way into the bowels of their laboratory quickly, Derek leading the way as I follow. He knows their additions to our prison better than I do.

The prison facility had been abandoned by our guards many years ago, but the humans had found it at some point, building a research facility over the buried prison and adding some of their more modern touches. There are plenty of things I don't recognize in the halls but there's no time to take it all in.

I have but two goals.

Kill the man who had kicked me and free my siblings.

I tell Derek as much and he seems to accept it.

"The guards should be busy with the others and I know where the Colonel is. Come on."

Good, very good. Derek shall be a useful tool.

We race towards the goals and I flex my fingers in anticipation. I do so enjoy mortal bloodshed from time to time…it's a vice, I admit.

Derek leads me to a room where a guard sits, watching images that move with the recognizable figures of my siblings. I see Kronos pacing his cell, enraged at being unable to leave. I see Oceanus attempting to batter his way through his door. They must have devices that relay these images to this guard, showing him what happens as it is happening. Curious.

The guard dies quickly, his neck snapped like a dry twig by my hands.

Derek vomits in the corner, so I ignore him for the moment, focusing on the images. I see that Iapetus, the one who gave rise to the mortals, besting several guards in an all-out brawl. He looks thin compared to the brother I remember. He still has some strength but it's not enough.

He falters as more guards come. He is far too weak to handle this many and they overpower him. The old guards of Tartarus had left weapons and tools behind, they will have to be destroyed or we can still be defeated. Titans are hard to kill but it's certainly not impossible. If they decided to use these weapons…best not to think about that.

I freeze in place when I see a newcomer in the image. The Colonel. At least that's what Derek had called him. A strange name.

The Colonel stands over Iapetus and gloats, I'm sure of that even though I cannot hear it. These images do not carry sound.

"Come!"

I sprint off and leave Derek behind, rounding corners until I reach the door. The door to Iapetus' cell. It is heavy, but I push it open, grinding the door on its track.

With it open, I find the Colonel!

No. No I don't.

It's empty. That is odd. Only Iapetus' body lays in the center of the room.

I wheel about when I hear it, but it is too late.

The door slides shut behind me, leaving me in this room. I shout and hammer on the door, but it is no good. The doors were built when I was at the peak of my of power and they will withstand it now just the same.

"Damn you!"

click

"Well done, Hyperion, well done. Didn't expect you would be so easy to manipulate but…here we are."

Derek. He and the Colonel stand in the guard post and stare down at the two Titans they have captured. Proud of themselves.

Fool! Me, not them. I should have known.

I should have known.

Damn.

Chapter III

I kneel by Iapetus, ignoring the laughter from the guards and our tormentors. He is thin and flat on his back. Our power does fade, and he appears weak. Very weak. Most of my siblings were in those images I saw before, though Iapetus looks worse than any other.

"Hyperion!" he groans, opening his eyes a little, "look how they fight back. I'm proud of them."

He winces as I move him to a wall, leaning his back against it.

"Furious and proud."

I can't help but laugh. I look around at the prison that I remember so well, identical in every way. I close my eyes and allow some of my energy to flow into his body, healing his wounds and strengthening him with what little I can spare. I might need the rest before long.

"Thank you, brother," he says, looking fractionally better. He stands with me and we both look up to the guard post where Derek looks…perturbed. He should be proud of himself, not perturbed. He tricked a Titan.

Even so, I will take perturbed.

It will do.

"Any ideas?"

Iapetus nods.

"One, now that we're together. Tethys is near, and I have a mortal under my sway. It nearly ended me brother, but I have him."

I perk up at that. If Iapetus has a plan, then it will certainly be a good one. He was always a clever one.

"What do you need from me?"

He looks to the guard room where both the Colonel and Derek stand, staring.

"I need you to do what you do best brother," he smiles weakly, "get mad."

It's an odd request from any of my siblings. Usually they demand the opposite. I spent my life being told to calm down. Now he asks this?

A smile pulls at the corners of my mouth.

But, who am I to deny this request?

"You will suffer until the end of time!" I roar it at the guard post, shaking the room with the volume of my voice, "you will burn for eternity until the flesh peels from your bones and you beg for the sweet release of death, but it shall never come!"

I use what energy I have left to bring forth a gout of searing flame that strikes the thick glass, with no effect. It does make the men stumble back though, which is something. The power of a god is unexpected when one has forgotten what gods can do.

As they reel, Iapetus closes his eyes and slumps, his mind leaving the room.

Somewhere in the facility a maintenance worker jolts from his magazine, standing slowly and retrieving a toolbox from his locker. He walks through the maze of corridors, avoiding the running guards and ignoring the shaking that rumbles through the facility. He makes his way into a room, swiping his badge for access. Inside are dozens of pipes that feed water through the facility.

He pauses, looking them over for a moment. Then he raises an arm to point at one of the pipes, before taking a wrench from the box and using it to turn a valve to the on position.

Then he leaves the room. Once he is out he shakes his head and looks around in confusion, before shrugging and heading back to the maintenance break room.

Iapetus opens his eyes as I continue to lash the walls and glass with fire, shouting ever more creative threats. With every *hiss* of fire on concrete, I feel my power fade.

"Brother, calm."

That's the request I'm more familiar with. I let the fire fade and take great heaving breaths. It is good he asks it of me. My power is almost spent.

"It is done." He says, letting his head fall back against the wall in apparent exhaustion.

Tethys sits in her cell and listens to the shaking and shouting, and even through the walls she knows who it is. She smiles at her brother, somehow, he must have gained access to his beautiful sun.

She leans back and wonders when they will come for her, it couldn't be long. Then she feels it. Flowing behind her. It had once before but they had quickly realized heir error.

Except it was back.

She placed her hand against the wall and she could feel it, despite the pipes and concrete she could feel it. It refreshed her. Empowered her. She drew the moisture from the walls, as much as she could.

She closed her eyes and took a deep breath.

"Soon, I will be there soon."

We wait patiently. Titans are one thing and that is patient. It's been thousands of years and patience is a virtue one must possess or else one will lose their mind. So, we sit.

It's different now, having someone to sit with. It is better, despite how weak he is. I never envied his source of power, it was hardest on him all these years. I could take some strength from the magma deep within the earth but very little. He had nothing.

He looks so old, not like the vibrant brother I once had. That infectious smile of his when his beloved mortals were off causing problems for the rest of us. I don't think any of us could love them the way he did. Without their belief and love in return, he is a husk of himself. No longer a tall, powerful young man with that infectious smile. He is bent with time and his long hair is gray and thinning. He leaned against the concrete with his eyes closed, breathing slowly and raggedly.

"Brother, stop staring. I don't need your eyes reminding me how I look."

He turns to me and smiles. I suppose it hasn't gone. Just the god around it.

I look up to see the Colonel and Derek still in the guard room, watching us with others. Men and women in the white coats and some guards. They are discussing something. Probably how best to enter the room and take us.

"I fear they will come before she does," I say to him. He laughs so hard he sinks into a coughing fit.

"Brother! Fear? The years have not been kind to me, but they have clearly ravaged you!"

I stare at him for a moment, but I can't help it. I start laughing too and we laugh until we need to lean on each other, sucking air in between fits.

"She will come," he says when we finally stop, "she must come."

I nod and place my hand on his. It is thin and bony and not at all like my brother's hand.

"She must come." I repeat quietly, staring up at the guard post. I smile and give them a little wave. They turn away.

How rude.

Chapter IV

Tethys looked around her cell, warily eyeing the two guards that watched her constantly. They had taken up staring when she'd sat against the wall but now they were back to whatever game they had been playing before. No discipline, she surmised, not like the old guards.

The shouting and shaking had stopped so either Hyperion was dead, or his power was exhausted. Either one was a good option with her brother. He had a temper to match the sun. As the cool water rushed through pipes behind the wall, she felt invigorated with each passing moment. Her fingertips brushed gently on the concrete and gathered beads of moisture to her hands.

She was lucky that they lacked discipline. If they had any then they would have seen her cheeks filling out, her hair thickening, her posture straightening. She felt at least two thousand years younger.

"How so few years can make such a difference," she said, giggling to herself.

She stood and stretched, feeling lithe again. She held out her hand and formed a small globe of water, holding it with great concentration above her palm. It shimmered and shifted there, glistening and perfect.

"Do you remember me?" she whispered to it. It formed itself into something like a wave, nodding its peaks at her, nuzzling into her palm as if some sort of pet.

"Yes, I've missed you too, but we have work to do." The water shot straight up into a column, intent and ready.

"Do you remember Hyperion?"

It slumped slightly but nodded again.

"I know, he was always very mean to you, but it has been almost three thousand years."

It didn't move for a few moments and then shimmied acceptance and went ramrod straight once more.

She saw that the guards had risen from their game in curiosity, pressing towards the glass of their viewing station as she spoke to her elemental.

"I need you to help him escape. Can you do that?"

She giggled at the column as it wobbled as if to say 'that's all?' and slid out of her hand to the floor, slithering along towards the door. It stood up as a column again for a moment, turning back to her for a moment before disappearing through the slimmest of cracks.

"The guards," she said after her trusted elemental.

The two guards were pointing, and one reached for something on his shoulder. There was a small shower of sparks from the box and then muffled screams. One of the guards was scratching at his face when he hit the viewing glass so hard it cracked. The other dropped to his knees and then out of sight entirely, also struggling at some unseen barrier on his face.

Then her elemental appeared on the ledge of the glass and shimmied again. Then the water was gone.

It slipped along the edge of a wall, looking like a simple underground leak. While two of the prison cells had been built to prevent those leaks in them, the rest hadn't. After all, only two Titans thrived on water. It paused at a corner, peeking just a tiny crest up to look around the corner. The facility was busy with guards and maintenance workers as they readied for the rest of the Titans, but it didn't care.

It was focused on the water bottle that a worker had set on the floor while they worked on a light fixture. Quickly it slunk to the bottle and made a pinprick hole with a quick jab, absorbing the water before slithering against the wall again.

"Damn it," the worker cursed, when he found his empty bottle, "'I'll be right back." He muttered something and stormed off. It followed him cautiously. The worker drove his shoulder into a door with the crude image of a man on it. It followed under the door.

Then it stopped.

The worker stood over a sink, running a tap of water into his bottle and cursing as it started a fine stream from the hole. It bounced slightly and quickly moved up the wall onto the counter, sliding down into the sink and under the running tap. The worker was busy holding the bottom of the bottle, cursing while trying to avoid the water stream. When he turned back around, it was far too late.

It slammed into him like a tidal wave, throwing the worker across the room into a stall door. He didn't move.

The column filled the bathroom to the ceiling, pulling from all three sinks.

"Hey, you alrig –"

The door opened, and a guard stood there, his mouth open. The column turned towards him as he took a step backward.

The worker in the hallway heard the scream and turned in time to see a guard being thrown into one of the walls by a rush of water. He didn't wait to see more, just dropped his tools and began running as fast as he could.

He did have the foresight to press an alarm button as he did. With that, the facility was filled with a siren and flashing red lights. The column stared at the lights before shrugging and quickly dropping to the floor, filling the entire hallway with water. A dozen guards splashed through towards the bathroom, pouring from an elevator. It rose up from the floor to their waists and each man stopped in confusion, one of them punching his hand through it to find air underneath the sheet of water.

A small tendril climbed the wall just as the guards realized what was happening. The tendril sank into the open light fixture and the hallway went dark.

I stand up at the sound of alarms, and glance to the guard room. They are panicked, looking to each other. The Colonel shouts orders that I can almost hear through the glass and the guards disappear. He and Derek have some sort of brief argument, Derek pointing at the two of us and the Colonel waving his arm towards the door.

They leave the room together and Iapetus and I are left alone.

"Do you think it's her?"

"Who else?" he says, coughing.

Our door begins to grind open and I draw what little flame I have left to my hands; what I wouldn't give for my damn chain. Iapetus tries to stand but falls to his knees and looks at me apologetically.

"It's okay brother, I will try."

It finally opens, revealing a column of water and a group of guards on the floor. It looks to me and then to Iapetus, rushing to his side. I can't blame it.

"Thank you," I say. It turns to me and nods slightly, then wraps itself around Iapetus and lifts him from the floor. It starts moving him towards the door.

"Yes, right," I leave the room first, stepping over the guards and checking the hallways. They are empty. I look back at the elemental and it points a tendril of water to the left hallway, so we go left. Two guards appear from a side room, but they are too slow. I snatch the first by the collar and lift him easily into the second with a satisfying *crunch* as skull connects with jaw. It sends both men sliding down the hallway in a heap.

We continue through the main hallway and the elemental directs me to the left again. It grabs at me just as I reach a small corridor and motions to a door. It gently eases Iapetus onto the floor again. Together we push on the door and it gives way, opening inward. When it finally reaches the end, I can't help but smile.

"Sister," I manage, before she is hanging from my neck. When she releases, she pats me on the cheek and smiles.

"Brother, I heard you making all that noise before. Three thousand years hasn't cooled your temper?"

"It has, blame that one for the outburst."

When Tethys sees Iapetus, she runs to his side. I look to the column of water and it looks to me.

"I'm sorry for… before. You did well, thank you."

It just shimmers and shifts and then bows towards me slightly and the waters calm ever so slightly. I suppose maybe we're friends now. As I turn, something wet slaps across the back of my head.

I look to find it turned away and shuffling around, feigning innocence, of course.

A smile tugs at my mouth, something I can't control. Perhaps just acquaintances for now.

Iapetus leans on Tethys and she recalls the water to her hand, the flood falling to the floor and leaving a small orb remaining, floating there.

"Well done, we may need you again."

It nuzzles her hand and then is absorbed.

She looks to me.

"So, where are the others and how do we get them out?"

Iapetus holds up a hand that stops me from speaking.

"I have an idea about that too."

We race together towards the central tower, I support Iapetus and Tethys leads on.

"Our luck won't last," I say. "The guards will figure things out. And soon."

Iapetus hobbles on weak legs beside me and jabs me in the side.

"Then hurry!"

Wonderful advice.

The prison facility was built around a central tower with two levels, the lower leading to the twelve corridors and heavy doors for each cell, and the upper level leading to the guard areas. These mortals had been working in here before they revealed themselves to us and had added their own halls and doors to various parts of their facility.

Iapetus guides us to a side room and our luck holds just long enough.

We rest him against the wall of the small side room with a large wheel in the center.

"They added this at my personal request," Iapetus explains, "it opens all the doors at once. Just in case they ever needed us urgently."

"Whatever caused them to disappear wasn't urgent?" I grip the wheel and begin to turn it, the old metal grinding and squealing as it resists.

"I fear that whatever caused them to stop coming came too quickly for them to do much of anything."

I glance at him and look to Tethys, who shrugs. I turn back to the task as footsteps close in, thumping heavily. Someone shouts.

"Stop them! Kill them if you have to!"

Tethys and I look to each other and she curses, drawing out the orb again.

"Any ideas?"

Iapetus lifts an arm weakly towards the wheel.

"I already told you, Hyperion, three thousand years and you still don't listen to your older brother. Not all our siblings are without power."

Right, I forgot. Only those of us who argued against the imprisonment were blocked from our power sources. Some took the punishment more willingly than I did.

I heave on the wheel with Tethys' help and we hear it, the satisfying sound of rust and age giving way to movement. The doors are open.

Our siblings are free.

Chapter V

It doesn't take long for the screaming to start, staccato *cracks* filling the air in rapid succession. I feel the facility shake with some unseen impact and it brings a smile to my face. The guards that had been coming for us retreat to a different level of the mortal facility, away from the pit of Tartarus. They shout and clamor as Tethys and I look out of the room to see a half dozen or more dragging their comrades away.

Brave. I can admire that.

The first one to come up the stairs is a handsome man with a short graying beard and hair the color of dark earth. His shoulders are broad, his fingers are thick and stained with dirt. A sickle is tucked into his belt.

"Kronos!" I shout. "Brother!"

"Hyperion! I should have known it would be you!" He smiles and lifts me with his thick arms easily. He looks as if he hasn't aged a day and I envy him for it. He had designed and built Tartarus, drawing deep on the earth and stone to craft our isolation cells. He could not escape his own prison, so he had been permitted a garden within his cell, one that maintained his physical power as he tilled the earth.

He seems to have forgiven me for our squabble of the past. I am thankful for that. I don't need to be remembered of the reason for this prison, since it is my doing.

The next Titan to come is a beautiful woman that latches on to his arm, smiling with her brother. She is my eldest sister, with long black hair that is pulled back tightly, and a twinkle in her eye. Her beloved pet follows her as always, crafted from molten rock. It is a majestic lion with a dull mane of red embers that pulse with heat and light.

"Rhea, sister, as radiant as ever." I kiss her once on each cheek while Tethys embraces Kronos.

"Little brother, as hot headed as always I assume," she says while returning them.

They are the oldest Titans. The first Titans, protectors of mortali-

Iapetus! I had forgotten in the excitement of the reunion.

"Quickly!" I lead them to our brother who weakly smiles at them.

"I'd get up but…"

He gestures to his shriveled legs that can no longer support his weight.

Kronos scoops Iapetus up in his arms and closes his eyes for a moment, allowing some of his energies to pass to Iapetus. I feel a twinge of jealousy over just how much power he still has.

When he sets Iapetus down, his legs no longer shake, and he stands slightly firmer than before. There are still more siblings to come from their cells.

Oceanus and Themis are next. Oceanus leans on Themis and I wouldn't recognize him but for the beard and hair. Both are thinned and so gray they are almost white. They are recognizable as his, impressive in their size and tangled mess.

He had been a massive man before, his beard something that rivalled the Northmen themselves. He is no longer that man, he has been long away from the sea. He was bent with what passes for age to a Titan. His muscles have become gaunt echoes of what they used to be.

"Quit yer gawkin'!" He snarls, then breaks into a crooked grin, "though I must look like something the sea forgot."

"Worse than that, even," I say. I don't interrupt as Tethys runs to her brother, she doesn't hang off him as she might have before, just grabs his face with both hands. They whisper to each other and we don't try to hear.

Themis is the smallest of us but even I am afraid of her temper, yet she calls it righteous justice. Her short hair is only a few finger lengths long and it suits her well. There is no weakness to her, her physical power comes from sources less elemental than some of us. She curtly nods, never one for reunions I suppose.

She sighs, letting her shoulders sag and she gives me a hug.

"It is good to see you brother," she whispers, a moment of softness before she returns to a face of granite and greets the others.

"The others?"

I ask it just as we hear the shouting.

"Help! Quickly!"

We spare no thoughts, simply run towards the voice.

Phoebe has never sounded so desperate.

We find her with Mnemosyne and Crius, standing in the doorway of one of the cells.

She is further in than the others and has dropped to a knee, holding out her hands towards him. His eyes betray madness, those once bright green eyes of Coeus are dull. He stands with his back against the far wall and warily watches all of us. His eyes dart back and forth but never settle on anything.

His walls are covered in writing from floor to ceiling.

The scars on his arms and legs are obvious. The ink he used was Titan's blood.

"Brother, please," Phoebe begs, "don't you remember?"

"Can't remember, can't. Not meant to, only forget," he stammers out. His voice isn't right either. We shouldn't have ever brought him here. He needed knowledge, to learn. Without it…

I look to Kronos and he looks at me.

I can see the shame in his eyes. His prison. His brother. I can also see the accusation, though he would never say it.

My fault.

Phoebe lets out a choking sob and runs to him, embracing him. He stiffens but does not retreat or fight, just stands there and does not embrace her in return.

"We have to go…" I hear my own voice and it surprises me, "if we don't go now we might be trapped down here for another three thousand years. Even Kronos can't dig us out from this deep."

Then it hits me. Eleven. I only count eleven.

I haven't seen her yet

"Where is Theia?"

Chapter VI

It doesn't take long to find her.

The medical rooms are close to our cells and the guards have retreated from them. I am told that I shouted for her for quite some time. I don't remember that. I just remember crashing through doors. Seeing her in that cold place without any semblance of warmth.

I also remember someone trying to hold me back and I remember driving my elbow into their nose.

Kronos was less than pleased about that.

It is a room that I remember, much like the one that I suffered in. Harsh bright lights and sterile walls, it's just missing the twisted men and women with scalpels and other assorted instruments of pain.

She is under those bright lights, not the sister I remember. She looks like herself, but she does not have the life that I remember.

She lies on a steel table, so still, so beautiful.

My twin sister doesn't move as I gently brush the golden hair from her face. She doesn't breathe. Her face is slack and peaceful, just as I remember it. Even after all these years.

My hands shake as I take one of hers in mine, it's so cold for a goddess of the sky.

I can't breathe.

I can't move.

When I finally remember to breathe it catches in my chest, escaping as a choked sob.

I take her in my arms, her head loosely rolling into my shoulder. I don't want to see the scars that cross her body. They must have come for her first.

Then they killed her. On a steel table without any of us to comfort her. To be with her in those last moments.

Did she scream? Did she beg for mercy? Did it hurt?

I kiss her forehead and let the tears come.

No one speaks, no one moves, they just look on.

I hold her and there is nothing more important to me at this moment. Nothing more important than where she needs to be.

"She deserves blue skies."

They part for me. Each of them gently caresses her as I go by, saying goodbye.

Iapetus and Kronos are last.

"They will try to stop us." Kronos speaks with gravity, he never succumbed to the same vices that I had. Spilling mortal blood was never an enjoyment for him. It comes easier for me when I am enraged.

That, admittedly, is more often than I care to admit.

I don't stop walking, still holding her. Somewhere beyond those doors is the stairwell to the outside. With sunlight and clear skies and escape. A place she deserves to see one last time.

Between us and that are men with weapons that can kill a Titan. That have already killed a Titan.

"You want to charge in against gods know how many men? Armed with gods know how many weapons from the armory? They've already killed one of us! Stop and think!"

He grips my arm tightly, squeezing with a strength that isn't inconsiderable. I stare at him, willing back the fire that would slam him into the wall. It must have reflected in my eyes. He releases my arm.

"We need a plan, not to charge at them. Look at where that got us."

He says it quietly to me and the weight of her body becomes almost unbearable.

I want to burn them all. I want to charge in and beat their skulls into dust with my bare hands. They all deserve to die, their flesh peeling from their bones as their blood boils to nothing but vapor.

He is right. Damn him, he's right. I take a deep breath and let the fire fade, those desires to fall away. Sometimes vengeance must be tempered with cold logic.

"A plan then," I say, "a plan."

Kronos seems pleased, relaxing. I realize then that he was holding the grip of his sickle, knuckles white.

"Save it for them," I say, nodding towards the unknown force that will align itself against us, "cut a path through them, or I will."

"If there are too many for you?" He asks. "Even the hottest fire can be quenched when enough blood is poured over it. Will we bury you here? Will our bones become the foundation of Tartarus?"

I flash my teeth at him. The image he conjures is striking, that much is certain.

"I don't want my bones to be a foundation for anything. If it is to be so then I will kill them all, or as many as I can. Then I will see Theia again."

Chapter VII

"**O**nly two ways out now, both are through us."

The Colonel said it with confidence. Derek didn't share that confidence.

"We just lost what, twenty guys down there? They opened all the cells; how did we not know about that?"

"Because I told my men to not just turn random wheels or cranks in a prison built for gods. It made sense at the time. Still does really."

The Colonel was a big man and Derek wanted to glare but it wasn't a fair fight. Corporate versus security, suit against thug. The Colonel looked at Derek out of the corner of his eye and his mouth curled up in a smirk.

"Go for it, kid. We'll see how that turns out."

Derek shook his head and turned his attention back to the guards that were taking up defensive positions. The main research facility had been built far above the prison, what they had come to know was the mythological Tartarus.

Not so much of a myth though.

Derek represented a corporate conglomeration with a vested interest in the prison and had sunk billions of dollars into the research facility. Their facility was staffed by hundreds of personnel. They had well-paid and trained guards, ex-military pilots, some of the best scientists in the world and an assortment of support staff.

The support staff and medical personnel were already evacuating out to the main atrium with a secondary guard team. The hangar and helipad were taking on the non-essential personnel and airlifting them out to the secondary facility at the base of the mountains. Derek would be leaving soon with them, corporate was not an essential position. He had a meeting to attend with their benefactor to explain what had gone wrong. A meeting he didn't look forward to.

"Go on then, son, tuck your tail and get lost. Let us handle it now." The Colonel continued smirking until Derek was gone.

"The Colonel" was a misnomer, he'd only been a Captain when he was still serving. Then a man from a big energy company had approached him with an offer and a generous pay bump. With that offer Captain Daniel

Richard became The Colonel, at least to his men.

He walked the first major defensive position and although he had hoped it wouldn't come to this, he always planned for the worst. That's why he had them take the armory first when they breached the prison proper. Before any medical facilities were built, he had designed everything in tandem with the architects. The facility had two entries, the main hangar and a duo of helipads. The helipads Derek had been instructed to lead Hyperion to. Though that plan wasn't supposed to end with...all this. Their benefactor was probably going to be unhappy. Scratch the probably.

Those two entries led into a massive atrium complex with several stairwells built into the mountain for secondary access but those had been sealed with a judicious application of expanding concrete foam. The route that Hyperion knew was no longer accessible to him and that was a small victory. With that there was a single massive tunnel serviced by an enormous elevator for moving equipment into the second facility. The top of the elevator was guarded by The Colonel's second-best team and the elevator could be shut down to slow them down.

That left another team of guards on the second level, where the main research rooms were located. A fully stocked medical bay with surgical theaters, additional holding cells that were intended to dampen the power of the Titans, guard barracks and guard armory. This is where Hyperion had been held before they had enacted the new plan. It had not been part of that plan to kill his sister nor for him and the others to be released. That was a small hiccup.

Now The Colonel and his men were securing the two choke points left in the facility. They were armed to the teeth with combat rifles and the fancy exo-suits that The Colonel still hadn't acquired a taste for. They made a man stronger and faster, but he had seen Hyperion summon fire and lost a small squad to a sheet of water that seemed to have the capacity for thought. Even if they were packing ammo reforged by their master smith using the weapons from the armories, they had to hit the Titans first.

Even though he wouldn't tell his men or really admit it fully to himself, The Colonel really wasn't sure he would win this fight. Not in close quarters. Not against Titans.

That didn't matter. They had a job to do.

"Ready up, they don't get past this point."

Some set their jaws and nodded, some lit cigarettes and took long drags to steady their nerves; others offered a quick prayer to whoever might be listening.

As if that would help.

Even as Titans we would have a difficult task of cutting through the mortals, only a few of us had any real power left and only Kronos had his weapon of choice. We needed our weapons to even the odds.

I gently laid Theia down and left her with Themis and Mnemosyne who promised to watch over her. Iapetus being as weak as he is, also stays. Coeus and Phoebe also stay given that Coeus isn't himself.

I worry he may never be again. His mind feels wrong. Shattered.

Tethys left on her own to scout any exits, she was the only one with the means to.

The rest of us went to the armories to find any weapons we could. If there were any left.

The first two guard armories were empty, racks that were once stocked with powerful weaponry now stood empty.

Crius is the first to speak.

"That's how they made tools and killed…"

I wince before he says her name and he stops under the withering glares of Oceanus and Kronos.

"How did they reforge those weapons? The smith passed his knowledge down for three thousand years?"

No one has answers, so we move to the last armory. This one Kronos had built in secret, much like Iapetus and his addition. Titans and their damned secrets. Kronos heaves at the heavy stone wall and I push beside him until it slowly pushed back to reveal what had been the Titan armory.

His shoulders sank at the empty room, twelve settings for Titanic weaponry that were now empty. His current sickle was a minor weapon compared to his original.

"Damn them!" Oceanus mustered some strength to kick at a rack in the center of the empty room. The weapons had power, power that some needed more than others. Rhea places a hand on his shoulder to calm him, a valiant attempt for our moody brother.

Kronos looks to me and raises an eyebrow.

"Brother, your chain was never stored here, you refused."

"I didn't trust them," I say simply. Titans, by nature, distrust mortals. Iapetus is the exception. We may love them, but we can't ever really trust them. Greedy little things that always seek more power or wealth or knowledge. Almost like Titans. I always thought they would betray us for power but instead they had apparently just died and been replaced with these heathens. At the back of the hidden armory was another heavy stone wall but this one had a spot that wouldn't be quite right.

I walk to it and run my hand along the wall for a moment, trying to remember where I'd put it. Then I feel it! The roughness of the wall is wrong in a small spot, no more the size of a fist. I motion for Kronos' sickle and he hands it to me. With the bladed tip I dig into the wall and carve out pieces, sending small stone chips to the floor. After a few moments I see it.

A black metal chain link protruding from the new depression I've created in the wall. I wrap my fingers through it and feel the surge of power coursing through each link.

"I've missed you," I whisper before taking a half step back and pulling on the first link with all my strength.

It comes from the wall, the length of a fully-grown man tearing free from the stone mixture I had made to hide my beloved chain. Chunks of rock fly through the room and pieces cling stubbornly to the chain. I whip it from one end and it snakes through the room, coming clean to reveal pure black metal. Metal forged of fire, fire from the sun herself.

Oceanus claps excitedly and gives me a weak slap across the back.

"Brother, I'm glad you were an untrusting prick back then."

I laugh, looping the chain over my shoulder and remembering the feel of it. The weight of it. The extension of my body. It is invigorating.

"As am I."

Titans and their damned secrets.

Two dozen guards stood watch at the choke point to the prison and lowest research facility, guarding the elevator shaft. They make idle chatter and grandiose claims about who would kill the most Titans when they tried to come up, nervous laughter rippling through them with each joke.

"Soldiers haven't changed, have they?" I say quietly to Tethys and she giggles softly. We are barely fifty feet from the group of guards who seem to be waiting for us to use the elevator. Not likely, do they think we're stupid? Some of us might be but Oceanus isn't making decisions at the moment.

They sound so different than the mortals I remember but there will be time to ask questions once we get out of this accursed prison.

Tethys' elemental carried us this far up the angled shaft until we found a good foothold, Kronos and Rhea are on the opposite side of the shaft where her elemental digs in with rocky claws. Four Titans against two dozen guards.

Hardly seems fair.

Tethys places her hand on my arm and pulls me from my thoughts.

"I'm sorry," she says quietly, a tear slipping down her cheek that she quickly wipes away.

"Me too."

Kronos waves a hand to get our attention and holds up the ball of earth he had been working with, nodding up towards the platform. He mimes throwing it and then points to each of us and then stabs that finger up towards the platform again. We all nod.

He holds up three fingers.

Two.

One.

The ball of earth sails up the shaft and the shouting begins. The staccato sounds start and then it stops.

"What was that?" someone shouts.

"Reload!" yet another voice.

"Griff, go check it out!"

We hear the footsteps approach the ball of dirt and Griff shouts back.

"Just…dirt!"

Kronos closes his eyes for a moment and focuses. Above us a group of guards close in on the ball with their weapons raised, at least half of them. It shudders with his focus raging through it and the outer shell becomes a dull metal color as it pushes all the projectiles to the surface. Griff's eyes open wide and he opens his mouth the shout his comrades to safety but it doesn't matter.

The ball explodes outward and sends their own projectiles outward with thunderous force, thudding into body armor like hammers and tossing the guards away as if they weighed nothing.

When the half that can get back up do they turn back to the shaft to see us. Mostly to see me.

I let the chain fall from one hand, the clanking links hitting the floor with the most satisfying sound. I stretch out my shoulders and pick one of the guards to stare at. I can almost see the lump in his throat and his hands have a slight tremor to them.

Excellent.

"Well, come on then." I say. Two of them come at me first, raising their weapons for a brute force attack. I flick the chain up and the end link strikes one in the chest, throwing him back into a concrete wall. He slides down and does not move.

The other finds himself with it wrapped around his ankle and with a pull he is on his back. I drag him towards me and hit him across the face with a closed fist. He also does not move.

Another raises his weapon towards me, I turn to deal with him but a lion of rock and fire crashes into him and they both skid across the floor while he screams. A group of them begin to fire their weapons at us but a screen of water rises, and the projectiles explode on impact, pieces drifting away harmlessly.

I see one that had been aimed for my head.

I also see the one who was aiming for me and he steps back nervously. Then he fires again and again, unsupported by his comrades now. He stops and the elemental collapses to the floor, returning the Tethys. He struggles with his weapon for a moment and looks up to see…

Me.

He winces and recoils.

I see Theia's face. I raise my fist, wrapped with the black metal to hit him.

His weapon hits the floor. He doesn't.

I lower my fist and breath heavily.

I want to.

She wouldn't have.

I feel Rhea's hand on my shoulder and even if she doesn't say it I hear it.

She would have been proud.

What few are left lay their weapons down, slowly. Very slowly.

"Good choice," Kronos says, "smartest thing you've all done so far."

The Colonel stands with a secondary team at the second bottleneck, checking over their weapons and making sure the non-essential personnel had been evacuated.

His radio crackles to life.

"Colonel, dear Colonel."

He closes his eyes and sighs, giving a quick motion to the men to begin their own evacuation procedure.

"Sorry but the Colonel is unavailable at the moment, I think he's buying flowers for your sister."

There is a long silence.

"I'll spare your men if they throw down their weapons but you, you I will enjoy killing."

"Good luck."

The Colonel tore his earpiece out and began shouting orders to his remaining men.

Chapter VIII

With the elevator under our control and information from the surrendering guards we are led to the final access point to the main facility and freedom. Most of the guards turn out to be in it for a paycheck. Makes sense really, after three thousand years without Titans or gods they wouldn't be there for us. Just a job.

They hadn't believed in all that.

Or at least they hadn't believed it before.

"How do we get out?" I ask one. He doesn't play tough guy, just answers.

"There's aircraft on the main level, with a pilot you can fly anywhere you want."

"You're still using aircraft?"

He gives me a queer look.

"Still?"

"Never mind, where can we find a pilot?"

No time for a mortal history lesson, perhaps they went back to fire being the greatest invention after we were imprisoned. Wouldn't surprise me, not one bit. They have clearly made leaps in some areas but others…not so much.

One of the men stands, shakily raising a hand.

"Excellent! That was easy. What is your name, mortal?"

"Jeff…my name is Jeff."

"Wonderful, welcome to the service of the Titans."

These mortals have been very busy. We had left our mortals with a great deal of advanced technology, but these ones had apparently taken more to warfare than travel or science. Each man wore a sturdy metal harness that made them stronger than their fragile bodies ever could be though still not nearly as strong as a Titan. They used rapid firing "rifles" that fire terrifically dangerous bullets, pointed and forged from the melted Titanic weaponry so they could injure or kill a Titan. Each guard also carried a knife reforged from the armory weapons.

Impressive.

Not that it had made any difference.

"There's another group of guards on the next level up," our new pilot informs us.

Tethys and Themis jog off to scout it out while the rest of us wait behind. I kneel by Theia and the guards don't make eye contact, probably for the best.

"It wasn't them," Iapetus says, his voice trembling again. His power is fading quickly, we will have to support him for some time.

"Don't be angry with them. Vengeance is called for, but it must be dealt to the right mortals. If it's not, then what have we learned down here?"

I don't speak for a long time. Then I look at him.

"Furious and proud, right brother?"

"Something like that." He puts a hand on Theia and closes his eyes. Then he stands and goes to talk to the captured guards.

Furious and proud. Only Iapetus could be proud of them still.

"They're not there, it's empty," Themis returns and announces it.

Tethys waits for us by the route to the main level, holding her orb.

She takes all of us up to the next point and her elemental is proven right, there is no one to be seen. They must have abandoned it when the first defensive position fell.

"Good, let's be free of this place then," Kronos says, motioning to Jeff to lead us to the hangar.

I still carry Theia's body as gingerly as I can as we wind through the halls and rooms, she is so close to the sky now. So close to her home.

Our pilot guides us to the aircraft and I am impressed. It's not anything like I remember the mortals having, not even close.

The black and white craft is blocky but still sleek in a way, painted to resemble snow and rock, or at least that's what it looks like. Two rotors are built on the side in circular and moveable pods and the tail sports two fins. He sits in the front and hits switches that bring the rotors to life.

"Impressive," Crius is thrilled by it, he always was the traveler. At least in the sky.

The craft lifts slightly and starts to turn its nose towards the other end of the hangar, deftly handled by our pilot. It's only then when I look at my siblings that I realize someone isn't with us.

"Where is Iapetus?"

The Colonel and his premier team of guards quickly roll out their secondary plan, two mobile anti-air batteries that will bring down the whole group. Their benefactor won't be pleased to lose all the Titans, but the Colonel wasn't asking permission and he certainly wasn't going to let all the Titans escape.

The Colonel waves to the Titans inside the craft then switches to a middle finger, spitting on the hangar floor in their general direction.

"Ready to fire?"

The men nod, the system is ready to engage. Anti-air missiles with metallic shrapnel stuffed inside their tips, shrapnel from the re-forged weapons.

He snaps his fingers and two of his men drag out a figure, throwing him down to the hangar floor. The Colonel saw Hyperion disappear into the cockpit of the craft, clearly shouting something and pointing down. The pilot shook his head and motioned to the anti-air batteries.

Hyperion reappears, and his face is contorted in absolute rage. The older one, Kronos does the same.

The Colonel smiles at them.

He gathers up a handful of Iapetus' hair and pulls his head all the way back.

And he slides a knife from the armory across the Titan's throat.

"No!"

I shout it and slam my hands on the door as Iapetus' blood drains from the gaping wound. He is calm as the aircraft starts towards the end of the hangar. He doesn't struggle or scream or fight. He simply stares at me and smiles sadly.

The blood pumps out and the light fades from his eyes.

With a final breath, our brother dies.

The Colonel lets go of the fistful of hair and Iapetus falls face forward with a thump, a pool of blood spreading out from his body. He wipes it on the back of Iapetus' shirt and sheaths the original Titan blade, turning to his men and giving an order.

The missiles leave a smoke trail as they fire from the batteries, taking direct aim at the aircraft racing down the length of the hangar. The pilot clenches his jaw tight and hits a switch that sends diversionary flares sprouting from the back of the aircraft but neither missile takes the bait in the enclosed space.

I am nearly tossed to the side as he maneuvers, his knuckles white on the controls.

"Little help?"

Phoebe grips Coeus' hand in hers and closes her eyes, Coeus just stares ahead and rocks in his seat. She mutters something and then opens her eyes again but gone are the beautiful blue pupils. Instead her eyes are a storm of grey and ice blue that roils as she continues her prayer. Her head tilts back and a pulsing wave emanates from her body into the hangar.

Everything stops around us.

The hands of time are still.

Iapetus' pooling blood stills from an ever-widening circle around his limp body.

The Colonel is still, his mouth open and arm raised towards our craft.

The missiles are still in the air, surrounded by flares that do not descend.

Nothing moves. Only us.

She holds this for a few moments and then crumples in her seat, Themis and Crius rushing to her. I squint as the brightness of the sun starts to build, she calls out to me.

Our pilot pulls on his controls and the craft takes a nearly vertical climb outside of the hangar entrance while the missiles harmlessly rocket off into the distance before slamming into a mountainside.

He levels it out and begins a hasty flight down the length of the mountains that I can recall, heading south and west towards the coast.

He looks at me and I give him a slight nod of approval. Then he looks down and takes a long, deep breath.

"That wasn't ass-puckering."

I don't laugh.

Even as the sunlight strikes me, and I can feel my power coming back once more, even as we escape our three-thousand-year prison. None of that feels celebratory now.

The mountain disappears behind us and we leave him – his body behind.

Oceanus holds Tethys as she cries into his shoulder. Kronos stands with me staring at the mountain that had been our home. Rhea holds Mnemosyne in her arms, Crius and Themis try to revive Phoebe and Coeus stares ahead.

He looks at me very suddenly, moving with jarring motion, eyes boring into mine.

"Did we kill the Titans? Can't remember. Can't forget."

Then he stares ahead again.

And I slump into a seat and scream into my hands.

Chapter IX

"They escaped?"

Derek swallowed hard and chewed his lower lip, dreading what came next.

Surprisingly, the large man took a deep breath that practically sucked all the oxygen from the room before sinking into his very expensive leather chair.

"Get out."

Derek obliged.

The man spun to look out the frosted glass of his office that overlooked a sprawling New York, templed his fingers and pressed them to his chin for a moment. He was a fit man that looked to be in his early sixties, even if he was a few years older than that. He lived a clean life and had always made the right choices to get to the top. He kept a neatly trimmed beard and short hair, both once a deep brown but now mostly grey. Under the cuff of his expensive and finely tailored blue suit was a tattoo that he now absently rubbed with his other hand.

He stood suddenly and fished his phone from his pocket and dialed a number from memory.

"Call the others, they escaped. Yeah, shit. I know. Just call everyone and get them here."

He struck the end button with a thick thumb and threw the phone on his desk.

Turning back to the window he returned his attention to the absent rubbing of the tattoo.

The black ink was older than most of the cities in the world, but no one would ever know that. He would simply take a new name and continue his reign of wealth and power. They would never know better. Money flowed and everyone around him was pliable.

Everyone.

They had always thought the tattoo was because of his position and company and it had even caught on with some of those around him in this life. There were some executives with matching ones which made switching to a new life much easier.

His would always be the original.

He looked down at it and smiled, drawing some comfort. If it was false bravado was to be determined.

"Let them come then."

Fixing his attention to a plan for the Titans he spared just one final thought about that tattoo. A thought of time.

He'd had the lightning bolt there for longer than he could remember.

We stand on the sandy shores of some secluded beach, far from the prying eyes of any mortals and taking a moment for ourselves. No chance to say a proper goodbye to our brother, but we could send Theia off.

Coeus was still staring blankly but Phoebe was looking much improved after her display of power. I often forget how strong she can be.

Crius and Oceanus were the last of us to be drained of power. Crius had quickly regained his once under a clear sky, drawing his power from the stars and constellations. Some of them hadn't been so hurt by the imprisonment, their powers were rooted in less physical needs than ours. Others had been devastated by the lengthened time in the prison.

Oceanus had quickly remedied his weakness as well by throwing himself headlong into the salt water. When he stood again, walking through ankle deep waters, he had quickly become himself again. He was no longer bent with frailty but standing taller than any of us. Wider too. His beard was again thick and pitch black like his hair and his crooked smile was still the same. Just livelier.

With that we were all ourselves again, just as I remembered us.

We were just two siblings short.

I carried Theia to a flat space not far down the coastline, all of us standing under a perfectly clear sky with a setting sun across the water. It was a brilliant sunset and the moon shared the sky as well.

"There's no better sky for her," Kronos says as I place her on the ground and brush her hair from her face. I kiss her forehead gently and step back to allow the others their moment of goodbye.

When they are done they form a circle around her, leaving two empty spaces. Then they all look to me. It is our first funeral for a Titan, but it feels right to say it this way.

I kneel beside her and kiss her forehead one last time before closing my eye and letting the fire of the sun pass from my body into hers.

The flames grow tall and consume her, turning a bright blue and reaching far into the darkening sky. Her ashes spread into the air and are lifted away on a gentle breeze. We stand a while longer even though her body is gone.

We say our last goodbye.

Iapetus. Theia.

Theia. Iapetus.

Kronos stares down at the rocks. I take his forearm and lead him down the water's edge, away from the others. We walk for a long time without speaking.

He stops very suddenly and takes my arm.

"Brother, I'm sorry. This is all my fault."

"That's why I wanted to walk with you."

He drops his head in shame.

"I was wrong you know," I say, continuing down the water's edge. He follows but doesn't speak.

"I remember our fight, I thought about it every day in that cell. I was wrong then. To think I was better than you. Than any of us. I wasn't. I'm not. I will always hate them for stealing Theia from me, always. But you were right, we had no right to wage war and involve the mortals. They are not toys or playthings for us, they are ours to protect. And ours to punish when they falter. I forgot that, back then. None of this is your fault, none of it."

He stops walking and stares out over the sea. When he looks back at me his eyes are hard again, they are the eyes of my brother once more.

"To punish."

I nod.

"Do you think they remember the Titans? Do you think they knew who was in that prison?"

"I don't know, brother."

He looks back out over the water.

"Then let's find out. And remind them just who the Titans are."

Our pilot was nervous, we'd left him sitting on the rocks near the aircraft and there he had remained. Kronos, Oceanus and I decided it was time for a chat.

"So, what do you know?"

"Probably not much but I'll tell you whatever I can," he was scared, eyes darting between each of us. Good.

"What year is it?" Mnemosyne interrupted us, coming and sitting in front of Jeff with crossed legs, "did you idiots forget I can read his mind? Coming over here with the whole big tough guy act, just ask him nicely and stop trying to intimidate him."

"Twenty thirty-six."

She took his hands.

"If you lie to me, I will walk away, and they will do what brutes do best. Got it?"

He nodded.

"Who sent you?"

"I just get paid, a guy I knew had this guy that he knew that was looking for pilots to ferry people in and out of there, that's all. Just a paycheck. I mean…who would believe it? I thought they were nuts when they talked about people down there, figured it was just rumors. The company that cuts the check is Orion Energy, some big US company in…well energy. I always figured there was some big discovery to be had down there for them, some reserve of oil or whatever. Then they shoved a rifle in my hands and told me to stop whatever came up that elevator shaft."

Orion Energy.

"What is the US?"

He gives us a strange look.

"Right, three thousand years…you've missed a lot. Oh!" he digs in his pocket, fishing out a flat object and tapping it a few times, lighting it up, "my phone. Connection's probably shit but it'll work."

Crius takes it. We would have gone to Coeus, but he is rocking back and forth and talking to himself, Phoebe desperately trying to bring him back to reality.

Crius sits with the pilot and Mnemosyne, learning how the little object works. All the knowledge of the mortals in such a small device. Dependent on a power supply. Fascinating.

Pretty simple now that I hear it, sort of astounding we didn't help the mortals with something similar all those years ago. It was the satellites, who would have thought of that? Not even Coeus would have launched anything *at* the sky and I suppose Theia and I just weren't clever enough to come up with that.

"Orion has a website, with profiles."

Crius is clearly picking it up well. He holds the phone and we all cluster around it, staring down as it comes to life with a picture. Piece by piece it reveals face. A familiar face.

There was a long silence. They slowly looked to me, as if I had answers.

I didn't.

Chapter X

The wind howls across the mountain but the cold does not bite into me, not with the warmth of the sun coursing through my veins.

The threat I currently face is different than the elements, however.

Kronos hits me across the mouth and I taste blood, coming back at him with a knee driven into his stomach. He sprawls out and gasps for air as I tumble on top of him, wrapping my chain around his throat. He elbows me in the gut, but I sink my knee into the small of his back and begin to pull, hearing the rewarding sound of him choking as the chain tightens.

That's when I feel it in my stomach, the point of his sickle slowly burying into my flesh. An impasse. Yet again.

"Brothers, stop!"

It is Iapetus and he is begging with us, pleading. His eyes are filled with tears and he points down the mountain. I fall back, letting the chain unravel from his neck. We both stare down at the fire and destruction. Cities burn even as torrential rain pounds down among the flames.

"Please. They are dying. They are dying for you."

I look at Kronos and feel shame. I have tried to kill my own brother for power and glory and he tried to kill me.

"For ten years they have marched armies in your names!" The tears come freely for Iapetus as he shouts at us, "We have begged you to stop and now they are dying by the millions! Babies have been slaughtered, children burned alive, family lines have been snuffed out for the two of you! How dare you!"

I see the others coming up the mountain as well. Themis is covered in dried blood and her eyes pierce through me. She demands something with those stern eyes. Justice. The fires eat at the mortal world and I see it. There is no justice for them. Not while we stand.

Kronos gets to his feet, dropping the sickle to the earth.

"We failed them," he says it quietly, so quietly I almost don't hear it.

"How do we make it right?" I ask Iapetus.

"You can't."

"We will imprison ourselves, the mortals will have time to recover and we will be punished for our crimes," Kronos says, holding himself straighter, "is that justice, sister?"

Themis nods.

"Then we shall do it."

"You two should be the only ones!" Oceanus shouts. "You want to take me away from my sea and from them because of your stupid feud?"

"Yes brother, they should find their own way for a time. We have been, all of us, too close to them. When they began to worship us, we should have ended it. Not embraced it."

"How long?" Kronos asks it of Themis, she is always fair in her decisions.

"One thousand years, an eternity for the mortals and a fitting punishment for us."

Punished. We don't deserve to be punished. We are gods. We-

Her hand touches my arm softly. As she does the skies begin to clear and the rain slows. She always brings clear skies wherever she goes, my sister. Her gift.

"Brother, no more."

I hesitate. She speaks it again.

"No more."

I look to the cities in flames and then to her. Then I agree.

"One thousand years."

Kronos builds his prison deep in the mountains where it shall remain, containing the twelve of us for one thousand years. He provides us with food and luxuries and enough books to occupy our time. Even for a thousand years.

Twelve mortals are selected to be our guardians, along with a small mountain town that will provide them with everything they need for our imprisonment. They will keep watch over the prison and pass down through the generations their knowledge until we are to be released.

Each of us selects a mortal that will be ours. They are friends of ours, ones that we have bonded with in these recent years.

One by one we enter our cells.

Crius, the youngest of us. The lad that loves the stars and gave the mortals navigation across the vast oceans. He winks as his door shuts first, looking to the constellations painted on the ceiling of his cell.

Coeus and Phoebe, the inseparable twins of knowledge and prophecy. Coeus with his bright green eyes and more books than the rest of us combined to keep his mind occupied.

"Won't be long at all, not with a good book." he says, giving his sister one last hug before his door closes behind him.

Phoebe is next, taking a deep breath before she steps into her cell. The one that lives every choice at every moment. Maybe this will be soothing for her.

Mnemosyne gives each of us a peck on the cheek and me a slap on the back of the head. Then a kiss on the cheek.

"My big brother. I'll remember you. All of you." She says and then her door is closed. She thinks she's funny, the one who doesn't forget.

Iapetus, knowing he will suffer the most, walks with surprising calmness.

As his door closes he smiles at us.

"Thank you."

Tethys and Oceanus, the latter grumbling, say their goodbyes to each other.

Oceanus offers a crude gesture as his door closes.

Tethys waves.

Theia and I have our moment together. She holds my hands in hers and gives me a kiss on the nose.

"Calm brother, perhaps some time down here will temper that fire."

I snort.

"Doubtful."

She laughs and then my sister is gone from me behind her heavy door.

Rhea and Kronos say their goodbyes and Rhea gives me a warm embrace.

"Try to listen to your sister," she whispers. Her door closes.

Themis doesn't say much, just a curt nod to each of us. Always fair, that one.

Only Kronos and I are left.

He walks to my door and sees me into the cell that will be my home for the next thousand years.

"We deserve this." He says.

I have nothing to add as my door closes and I am left alone. I stand in the center for a while before I am roused from my thoughts.

click

"It's just a thousand years, at least you have me to talk to. For a while."

I turn to look up at the guard room where he stands, offering a smile. I snort again and wave him off.

"I should have picked some better suited to conversation then."

He laughs, and the just sentence begins.

"So," I say, settling against the wall and looking up to him, "what are we going to talk about?"

"I suppose we can start anywhere, got nothing but time, right?"

"Thank you, Zeus," I say with a sigh, "for that reminder. Nothing but time."

XI

"I don't understand," I am looking at the face of my hand-picked guardian, "Zeus died. New guards came and everything, they told me he was just gone one morning."

"That's how they knew everything," Kronos says, sinking to the rocky ground, "I told Demeter about our weapons. I told her if anything were to happen where they absolutely needed us then we would need those weapons. I told her everything. I trusted her. She had to have turned on us."

No one can speak. Each of us is remembering our guardians. Our handpicked mortals that we spent the first years of our sentence with. Would they have all betrayed us?

Crius doesn't look up from the phone and our new pilot looks positively confused.

"It's not just him. Orion has partnerships."

He holds the phone up again. Oceanus' face is crestfallen. He and Poseidon had been so close, they'd sailed together on the oceans and shared a love of the sea. They had been friends. Now the man was in pictures in front of giant ships, a trident tattooed on his arm and a global shipping company to his name.

"Poseidon, that bastard!" Oceanus roars, losing himself to the rage. "He destroyed my hammer! Turned it into a damned dinner fork!"

He's not wrong. In one picture, the man we know as Poseidon sits behind a large wooden desk and smiles. He sits under an ornate golden trident with blue metallic veins running through the handle. Any of us would recognize Oceanus' ship building hammer, even reforged like that.

"You mean..." Jeff speaks and then stops when he sees us staring, but Mnemosyne motions for him to go on, "you mean the myths are real? I mean, you keep saying Titans, but I figured that was just a thing you called yourselves...but Zeus and Poseidon I know."

"Myths? Wait, you know them?"

"Oh man," he tugs the phone from Crius' hands and quickly types something in, "you guys are going to lose it. Watch this video."

We gather around and watch the small screen.

"The Titanomachy was a ten-year war between the Olympians and the Titans, where the god Zeus and his allies cast down the Titans from their rule and into the prison of Tartarus. Zeus, son of Kronos and Rhea…"

"That shit! That's disgusting!"

A surprising curse from Rhea, though she's right about the disgusting level of it. Brothers and sisters consorting? Unimaginable.

"-allied with his siblings and the formerly imprisoned Cyclopes and the Hecatonchires, waged a war against his father. The Cyclopes forged great weapons that the Olympians used to defeat the Titans…"

"We never imprisoned the Cyclopes," Phoebe said this, she'd always been very fond of them, "and they would never make weapons against us."

Jeff gave her a queer look but didn't speak.

"Enough, enough. It's all wrong but I think we get your point."

He shuts off the video.

"What do we do now?" Mnemosyne asks it quietly, "they have our weapons, they rewrote history, they wiped us from existence. No one will remember us, no one will help us. Except him."

"Siblings. That video said siblings. We don't even know for certain if Demeter was part of it but that probably means it's more than just Zeus and Poseidon. Either they killed the others or convinced them to join the betrayal."

Tethys' voice betrays her pain and I give her the best comforting smile I can, even if it's not my strength. I know how much she had loved her guardian, they had always been racing each other and he was always winning.

"I know what we need to do next." Oceanus speaks, and loudly. "This one flies us to wherever we can find the fool that stole my hammer and we make him talk. And then I'm going to shove that damned three-pronged monstrosity right up his..."

"He's not wrong," Kronos says, "he has answers and he has one of the Titanic weapons. We need both. Besides, they remember us as we were three thousand years ago...they would expect Hyperion to come for Zeus."

He's not wrong.

That *was* going to be my suggestion.

Though doing the unexpected may be in our favor over my vengeance. We all deserve that now.

"Alright." I say, "let's visit an old friend."

"They escaped? Billions of dollars and hundreds of personnel and you managed to royally cock it up, didn't you?"

The Colonel doesn't flinch at the man shouting at him, just wiped a bit of flying spit from his cheek.

"Sit down."

Poseidon thumps down into his seat at the conference table, crossing his thick arms with the trident tattoo in blue ink on his right forearm, sparing glares for both The Colonel and Zeus.

Only six chairs were filled and that was all that would be. Zeus cursed his compatriots but refused to let it crack him, not that any of them would have been much help. He only knew where Aphrodite was, but she wasn't taking his calls and he didn't expect she ever would, not from him. They'd had a rough relationship even before he announced his intention to open Tartarus.

The others had started disappearing long before that, they had just never been comfortable with the situation.

"So, what do we do?" Demeter asked, rubbing the bridge of her nose between her thumb and forefinger.

"Kill 'em."

Demeter rolled her eyes at Ares, the former being the much more rational.

"That's always your solution. Let's just kill them, kill those ones too. Kill, kill, kill."

Ares shrugged.

"Yeah. It works. Should have killed them back then but someone decided we could just leave them there. *'They'll never get out,'* I remember you saying. *'No need to put ourselves at risk. Just take their power and become the new gods.'* Remember that? I remember that."

"Damn good thing we didn't kill them, don't you take to forgetting just why we were going back for them," Zeus jabbed a finger at Ares, who slapped it away.

"We need a plan." Hera silenced the brewing fight. "Even without their weapons they won't be easy to stop."

The Colonel cleared his throat and Derek shot an elbow into his side, but the man stepped forward.

"Hyperion has his chain."

The collective group groaned in unison.

Dionysus stood.

"Well, I'm not sticking around for what comes next," he said, unscrewing the top of his flask and taking a long drink. "And I suggest you all do the same."

Then he was gone, leaving behind a slamming door and nothing else.

"The most violent and angry of them has his weapon, is that right? How did that not get taken?"

Zeus and the others all stared at Ares, who was responsible for the outburst.

"I don't know, why don't you explain that one yourself? You were responsible for gathering everything, you said it was handled. How did *you* miss it?"

Ares clenched his jaw and stood, leaning on the table with both hands.

"It was handled, the damn thing wasn't anywhere in that prison!"

Zeus rubbed his temples.

"No matter, one of them has his weapon. We still have the rest and we can still kill the others. What about the weapons we forged from the armories for you?"

The Colonel stepped forward again.

"Still in our hands, they didn't take anything but the VTOL."

"Good," Zeus clapped his hands together loudly, "however much you need you will have, right?"

Poseidon and Demeter nodded, they were the only other billionaires at the table after all.

"I'll get more men," Ares said, straightening his tie and buttoning up his suit jacket, "as many as you need. We'll finish it, how we should have finished it back then. Instead of letting it become a damned runaway train."

Ares left with The Colonel close on his heels.

Zeus, Hera, Demeter and Poseidon were left. They sat in silence.

"Do you think they know it was us?" Demeter finally spoke.

"If they don't yet they probably will soon. They have a human with them after all. If he knows any of the rumors of who sponsored the facility, then they'll know soon."

Zeus turned to look out the window again.

"They'll come for me first, especially if it's Hyperion that has his weapon. He'll want revenge once he knows it was me. I'll go to Olympus. It's as secure as anywhere else in the world. The rest of you take on tracking them, try to stop them before they get to me."

Demeter and Poseidon nodded and left, leaving just Zeus and Hera.

"You want me to stay?"

"No, can't take that chance. If he kills me he might stop."

"You know that's not true. Poor Theia, I should have been there to stop them."

She stood there for a long time and then when he didn't move, didn't speak again, she slowly left. Quietly shutting the conference doors behind her.

That left Zeus staring out the window, wondering to his own fate.

They should have killed them back then. At least some of them. Too late for that now. He took a deep breath and tried to think about how it would work out. There was no answer. He offered one last thought to the empty room.

"Shit."

Ares and The Colonel stood in the elevator, going down to the lobby. Ares looked to the man he had recruited.

"Do you think they know?"

The Colonel scratched at his arm aggressively and shook his head.

"This skin is wrong, feels weird and smells funny. No, they don't know. How would they?"

Ares shrugged.

"I don't know, okay, they've beaten us at every turn so far."

The Colonel rounds on Ares and slapped him.

"They have not beaten us! Those idiots started a war and they will again, if Zeus hadn't gone back to that prison nothing would have changed and no one would have been the wiser! Mistakes have been made but they will come, Hyperion will kill Zeus and then we will kill them. All of them. I won't let them drag the world into another war, not like that."

Ares straightened as the doors slid open with a *ping* announcing the ground floor.

The Colonel shook his head and looked at his hands, turning them over with disgust on his face.

"I want a new body, this one feels too tight."

They walked together to a waiting car sandwiched between two others that were packed with private bodyguards. Ares ran a very successful private contracting firm with government ties, giving him access to some very nice perks.

He opened the door and stood back for The Colonel to slide into the back seat, Ares followed behind him.

Neither saw the pair of eyes that watched them from a distance and took note.

No one did.

Chapter XII

I sit in one of the seats and watch my siblings.

Themis and Mnemosyne found Poseidon's headquarters and office in a city called Singapore, a heavily populated city where his shipping company had found an enormous market.

"Did you see this?" Themis holds out the phone. "Articles questioning how his company got to be so big in the past decade. One of his competitors lost three vessels in one month to freak storms, another one lost two the next. He's become a lucky charm to his clients and it's made him very rich. I found this too."

She dragged her finger across the screen to another series of news articles. She had taken to the technology much like Crius had.

"His shipping helped launch another business in Argentina, an agricultural conglomerate that just happened to have some of the most fertile crop harvests that year while others suffered. Run by this woman."

I don't think I've ever seen Kronos' jaw so tightly set. For a moment I worry he might crack one of his teeth.

"That traitorous swine, I'll gut her."

"It gets worse. I found Dionysus too, he's in Russia running nightclubs. And Hera is married to Zeus, though she runs some sort of medical facility. They're all linked together, feeding off one another."

Mnemosyne looked at the picture of her close friend and winced - he was hanging off two beautiful women with a half empty bottle of alcohol in each hand. Hera was more respectable looking in her pictures, wearing a white coat.

Rhea didn't look. She would be the most hurt out of any of us. Rhea and Hera were like family. Everyone was family to Rhea.

"What about the others?"

Themis shook her head and went back to the phone. Phoebe was still sitting with Coeus, trying to get him to talk but he just stared ahead blankly. Crius was sleeping on some of the seats towards the back of the craft. No one wanted to talk about it.

We'd left his body behind and it wasn't right, but we couldn't go back. Not like they would leave a Titan's body there anyway. The facility was useless without us.

I stand and go to the cockpit to watch the coastline drift by as we fly incredibly low.

"Gotta avoid radar," our pilot says, "can't get spotted now."

I sit and stare.

"Can I ask you something?"

The pilot, Jeff it was, pulls me from my reverie.

"Yes."

"What are you going to do? When all this is over I mean."

I look out the window again and close my eyes for a moment and remember Iapetus and Theia, their hopes for the mortals. Their faith.

"I will try to do it right this time."

"What's our plan then?"

I smile at him. Mnemosyne says he's a good sort, didn't believe any of the stuff about gods right up until the last few hours when it was hard to deny. He had three little girls he needed to provide for and a wife that loved him enough to let him take a job halfway around the world.

Apparently, he made a very delightful lasagna.

Whatever that is.

She'd spent some time prodding his mind to be sure he wasn't going to turn on us.

"Our?"

He shrugs and shoots me a sideways glance.

"I'm not big on the god stuff but you're real enough. And I guess you all seem decent, you could have killed everyone back there. Especially after…all that. You didn't though, so I figure I'll help you out. Plus, it keeps me alive. And I like being alive."

I don't say anything.

"If that's alright with you of course."

"I appreciate it."

There's more silence.

"I'm sorry about your sister and brother."

"Me too," I go back to staring out at the coastline, "me too."

It becomes mesmerizing and soon I drift into sleep.

Her smile is bright and infectious, even then. The sky is clear, and the sun shines brightly on green fields and small huts. The mortals move about their days and wave, enjoying the warmth that brings their fields to life.

She kneels and scoops a small green bud from the ground and hands it to me, buried in a fistful of earth.

"Bury it brother, it can be yours!"

She laughs and joins a group in watching Kronos and his farmers work a plow through one of the fields. I see Coeus with a group excitedly writing on a piece of slate and sharing it with them, some formula or idea that's come into that mind of his. Themis scolds a little boy who has stolen from his friend, pinches his ear and then sends them on their way to the river where Tethys, always playful, calls them over. A column of water shoves the boys into safe shallows and their laughter fills the air.

Oceanus heaves an enormous plank by himself, earning impressed looks from the men that help with the dock construction. They clap and cheer as he carries it through the shallow water along the beach edge and lays it out along the edge of the dock. He bows, and his laugh is louder than anything in calm midday breeze.

Crius is plotting out a course with experienced and novice navigators, men that will soon take a voyage onto the oceans to explore distant lands. He shows them Coeus' device that will help them gauge distance by the stars.

Mnemosyne and Rhea sit with the mothers and their babes, Mnemosyne telling a story that enthralls the youngest children and Rhea, a gentle one, that soothes crying babes.

Kronos had been right to pull the earth into their form, Iapetus had been right to give them life.

He watches from his hill, ever content to simply exist among these mortals. They will die but they will live. A gift even if it has an end.

Phoebe's hand touches my shoulder and I turn to her.

I recoil; her face is blackened and sags, dripping with ethereal ooze. She looks at me with eyes that are as black as night. Black blood pours from her mouth when she speaks.

"Death will come."

Thunder roars and the sky turns black, the sun is blotted out as tendrils of soil creep up from below and ensnare my feet. I see the others, but they walk freely. They are not themselves. They are hollow and cold and make a circle around me, chanting something. The same black blood drips and seeps from their mouths and eyes and ears.

It's a hissing word that I can't make out. The mud claws up my legs and torso, pulling my arms down. I strike with my chain, but I have no fire, no power left. I am drained as the mud claws my arms down and then my neck and begins to claw into my throat.

I can't breathe. I can't move.

She stands near me, shoulders sagging with some burden. She looks to me. My sister.

They all shriek the word and surge forward, sinking dark blades into her body. She screams and disappears under a seething mass of arms rising and falling as her blood cascades through the air.

I try to scream but no noise comes out.

They leave her lying there and come towards me, raising their blades, screaming and shrieking as their arms descend towards me and-

I sit up in the seat and scream. I am in the cockpit again and Jeff is staring at me with panicked concern, leaning as far away as he can.

"Um…are you okay?" he says, visibly relieved when Kronos rushes into the cockpit.

"What happened?"

I rub my eyes and force the dream away, trying to forget their faces.

"Just a dream," I say, "just a dream."

I stop. Kronos stares, Jeff watches me carefully from the corner of his eye.

"No…"

I remember that day. Iapetus had given life to Kronos' forms and the mortals had become our wards, the village had grown quickly and that was where everything had started. That was the day we became gods to them. It wasn't a dream. It had happened. Not all of it but I remember that day.

"Phoebe."

I push past Kronos and out to the others, where they stare at me, except Phoebe. She looks down at the floor. I grab her by the shoulders and she looks up slowly, into my eyes.

"You knew?"

She closes her eyes and the tears squeeze out past her eyelids to drop to the metal floor.

"I know everything brother, everything that can come and has been is happening now. All at once."

"No!" I shout it, "you knew *she* would die!"

She doesn't speak.

"Why? Why would you let it happen?"

"Thanatos."

The word. That word. They screamed it over and over again as they cut her. It hadn't come from Phoebe. Not her. Coeus. His eyes are distant, but he looks at me, or through me, maybe both.

"Thanatos. Death."

Coeus goes back to staring at the wall. Phoebe sits and cries.

"Why, Phoebe?"

She opens her eyes and looks into mine. As if there is nothing else.

"Because we cannot change our fates. And we are fated for death."

Chapter XIII

We sit in a long silence until Jeff interrupts it.

"We need to stop. We either need to find an airfield with some fuel or we need to get ready for a less than pleasant landing."

"Where are we?"

"Egypt, there's a small airfield not far from here that might be good enough. If it's not…well it's a long walk to Singapore from there."

"Do we have a choice?"

"Always a choice, in this case it's a difference in the quality of the landing."

When we land Jeff opens the side doors to the craft but only Kronos and I get out with him. The airfield is a dusty strip with a metal roofed building and small tower beside it. There's two large cylinders tucked behind the squat building and a handful of lights behind rusty metal cages.

We approach, hearing laughter inside the building.

"Military trucks," Jeff whispers, pointing to two large vehicles to the side of the building, "try to be careful."

Before either of us can speak the door swings open and a man stumbles out into the night, illuminated by the caged lights. He wanders to the side of the building and unzips his pants.

In the middle of carrying out his business he sweeps his head and his eyes settle on the three men coming towards the building in the night. I can see how it must look. One wearing a uniform. The others carrying a sickle and chain.

That cannot look good.

He shouts something that sounds vaguely like an alarm and struggles with a weapon on his hip, drawing it out and shakily aiming at us. A moment later the door bursts open and men pour out into the night, most carrying rifles.

"Jeff, please leave."

"Yup."

He slowly backs away and disappears into the night.

"We just want some fuel!" I say, raising my hands and stepping forward slowly, "that's all. No trouble."

"Trouble?" One of them gives a grin that's missing more than a few teeth, "Trouble."

Excellent.

They open fire. Their rifles spew flame from the end and bullets fill the air. I feel each impact, a dull thudding against my chest and legs and arms. One hits my forehead. When they are done Kronos and I still stand. They do not have the forged ammunition.

"Trouble, then."

I flick the chain and the end knocks out any teeth that the speaker had left, his body crumpling against the building. Kronos is faster and closes the gap, slashing with his sickle across two of them. They scream and fall to the ground. Before he moves again I wrap two in the chain and send a burst of flame along its length, engulfing them in blue fire.

Kronos picks one up by his collar and tosses him into the wooden tower with a sickening *crunch* of bone on wood. The last two flee to a truck and it roars to life, trundling down the roadway and gaining speed. It suddenly stops, metal crumpling and glass shattering in the night.

Water slithers towards us and leaps into Tethys' hands.

"Subtle," she says mockingly.

A shot echoes in the night and another soldier drops, he had been fleeing out the back of the building.

Jeff stands from his kneeling position and offers an awkward smile.

"If they get away they talk, they talk, and we get caught. At this point I'm sort of in for a penny in for a pound. Fuel?"

When we are airborne again, Kronos rubs at some dried blood that covers his knuckles. As he scrapes it away, Phoebe looks to him and then to me.

"We are fated for death. Ours or theirs. It always leads to death."

Zeus stood in his second office, this one in a complex his company had built in New York State, a sprawling facility that technically housed their research and development arm. It did house research but not the energy kind. There was not much in that field that Zeus didn't know about already.

The development was unique. Or had been.

The Smith was gone, and he'd taken the damn Cyclopes with him.

Nothing was going right for him now, not since the Titans had escaped because of some idiotic plan to empower one for more valuable study. He had told them not to let any of them near their sources of power. He should have been there. If he'd had the chain from the beginning maybe none of this would have had to happen.

It was too late for all that.

He turned as his door opened.

"Sir, the Egyptian authorities are reporting a squad of soldiers has been killed at an airfield. They're putting it down to local militants but… "

"-it's them. Let Ares know, maybe his men can intercept them before they disappear. It's only a matter of time."

Derek nodded and left. Zeus was reminded of himself when he looked at the younger man. That was the point though. If they looked too different it wouldn't work. Immortality in the modern era had become so complicated with photographs and media coverage. He couldn't just slip under the radar anymore. Now he had to raise up some young executive that would eventually replace him and when the time was right he would slide into their place, with their name and his legacy would continue.

It had worked so far, though a few times he had come close to being revealed. Money did wonders for some. Others disappeared.

He took a few steps and locked the door to his office, walking to the wall and removing a rather large and flattering painting of the Olympians that he had become fond of. Behind was a large black safe. He entered the combination and rested his palm on the scanner, rewarded with the sound of the safe unlocking.

He slowly opened the door, bathed in pulsing blue light. There was only one bolt in the safe. There was only one bolt left. He shut the safe again, comforted by the sight of his remaining power.

He needed more. He had some of his men tracking the Smith but that was a temporary fix, he needed the chain. He needed Hyperion dead.

It would be his. The Titans would underestimate them, they could never see power beyond their own. That was their flaw.

"The sky is my domain now," he said to no one in particular, staring out over the compound. "Come and take it."

Chapter XIV

I am amazed at what these mortals have accomplished in the three thousand years we've been gone. We had given them so much but to see what they have done without our help would have made Iapetus so happy.

If only he could see them now.

They cover the world now, billions of mortal souls spread over nearly every inch of it. Just astounding.

Our pilot informed us that it would be safer to "ditch the ride" and find new transport before they started tracking us. Oceanus and Crius voted on a ship and the rest of us went with it. It was harder to track and would give us some time to craft a plan. We landed near a city called Djibouti.

Some things never change, though the mortals may span the globe and construct enormous cities there are some universal truths that remain as they were.

Mortals are inherently greedy.

Not always for tangible wealth. Sometimes they seek something more substantial to their very souls but, it has always, and likely will always be a truth. Power, wealth, fame, a sense of pride. Mortals crave those.

Mnemosyne and memories go hand in hand. The key to her is that the memories don't have to be real, she can create them. She found a shipping captain and planted the seeds that we had already purchased passage with him. That is how we found ourselves bunking on a massive shipping vessel and rocking through the ocean on our way to Poseidon.

Oceanus was obviously thrilled, spending all his time on the deck with the crew and granting what little power he could to the speed of the ship. It's not very thrilling, I admit, sitting in the bowels of a ship and making our way to a new city. To find a god.

It did however grant a moment to stop. To think. Only a moment.

I sit on a thin mattress when one of the crew throws a pile of clothes at me with a heavy thud. I look down at my own dirty, torn clothes and realize how truly disgusting I must look. Not very god-like at all.

Even clothes made by gods can only last so long and three thousand years is past that limit.

There are water stained mirrors and functional showers on the ship. I strip down and wash, the desert dirt pouring down the drain with the warm water. There is dried blood under my fingernails from the fighting that I dig out until I feel clean again.

I stare at myself in the mirror, tilting my head and looking at a man I barely recognize. He is young looking, not like the man in the cell, his hair is dark and thick and there is scruff along his jaw. His amber eyes seem distant, as if they are lost somewhere a thousand miles away.

I rub his jawline and point at him and he points at me.

"You need to shave."

I step out and Tethys whistles, slapping my cheek as she goes to the stalls for her own shower.

"Our brother, all cleaned up."

One by one they leave and return, each time looking more like a Titan and not some grungy desert rats that have been on the run. Though that's almost entirely what we were.

"The prison feels like an eternity ago now, doesn't it?" Themis sits beside me, her serious face gone for the moment. She runs a hand through her short hair and spikes it up.

"Three thousand years wiped out in a whole two days, seems right. Like it never even happened. Were we ever even in that place?"

She lets out a short laugh, the most I think I've ever heard from her.

"Hyperion," the serious face is back, "do you think we can do this?"

I've never heard Themis like this.

"Yes, we can. We're gods."

She shakes her head and looks at the ship's deck.

"We were gods. We're not now."

The silence hangs there while I try to think of an answer, something good to say back. She's right though. We were gods. Now we're rusty and beaten down and mostly weaponless Titans in a world that doesn't remember us. If they do it's as the myths that Zeus and the others seem to have peddled in our absence.

"We were gods."

Even with our powers back we weren't some formidable force yet. And they had the weapons to kill a Titan, having already done so twice.

"Themis," I said it quietly, "should we have just…you know."

"No, it was time for us to return. Find out what the world is like without us. Maybe it's better."

She rubs her palm idly.

"I hope it's better." She says it and I almost don't hear it.

"If it's not? What if they've become some perverted form of what we intended? What we were put here to make them?"

"Then we start over."

I look at the chain and think back to the days before Kronos crafted the clay and the sky gave it life. The beginning of everything. How we watched them grow before our eyes into the mortal race that we served. That had betrayed us now. Some of them had.

"I'd like to vote no on that."

I look at Jeff and snort. He's growing on me.

I lay on the bed and close my eyes, letting the rocking of the ship carry me to sleep. We still have a week before we'll arrive at Singapore. Plenty of time for us to get ready.

And time for them as well.

Chapter XV

Singapore was a major shipping port and Poseidon had capitalized on that, moving his company to the burgeoning city years ago. He had built an empire on the rusted hulks of his competitors that always seemed to befall some unfortunate catastrophe at the right time to keep him on top. His office was ostentatious compared to Zeus, who had always been the more modest of the two. If that was saying anything.

He had a desk that was carved from the wood of a ship lost at sea and long forgotten, by all but him. The first ship that he had sunk to begin his empire. He was the Olympian that had bought into his own mythos, far more than any of the others. God of the Sea.

He had decorated his office with ornate model ships through the years and hung the golden trident over his desk. When the press had come knocking to interview the "king of shipping" he had taken a picture behind that desk, right under the trident. It had become something of a joke in the community.

Though "eccentric billionaire" was no longer a rarity.

His offices were near the sea, as he had wanted them to be, a tower with half the floors devoted to his many employees that coordinated shipping routes and times, tracked cargo and delivered good and bad news to him.

He smiled at himself.

His ships were always faster than the competition. Always. Controlling the seas will have that effect.

"That fool should have never gone back to Tartarus."

His lackey looked up from some financial reports, raising an eyebrow.

"Sir?"

"Zeus. He should have left them to rot down there, not opened the doors. Some great plan."

He snorted and eased his ever-widening girth into the chair, wincing at the creaking noises it made. He was getting fat. He looked down and pinched a roll together and grimaced. He'd have to make some time in his schedule for the gym.

"Sir, can I ask why he even wanted to go back there?"

Poseidon looked at the young man and envied his slim stature.

"He wanted to live forever, of course."

The man didn't seem satisfied, and Poseidon sighed.

"When we took power from them it was through their weapons and tools. That's the only way we could become like them. Zeus couldn't find Hyperion's chain, so we each sacrificed a small piece of our weapons for him and those pieces were smithed together to give him a god's life span."

He looked to the trident, where he had asked the smith to leave a reminder that it was not whole. A small imperfection in the center prong.

"It worked for almost three thousand years, but Zeus was never as strong as he made himself out to be. He relied on the lightning made by others and the fact that his power came from so many sources, it gave him broad strengths rather than focused ones. True power is broad. Great power is direct."

The young man nodded along.

"Why help him?"

Poseidon furrowed his brow.

"He's my brother."

"Not really. He's just some guy lording his power over you, power you gave him, while he looks to gain more. Don't buy into your own myths."

He went back to the financial reports and Poseidon was left to think about that. While a bit of an upstart thing to say the boy wasn't wrong.

Zeus and Poseidon weren't brothers. They had just been watchers of Tartarus once. Co-conspirators maybe, but not blood. Maybe it was time for a change. He could pull some of his men away from Zeus, leave a gap for the Titans to slip through. They were smart, they could figure it out.

Yes.

Maybe it was time for a new Olympian to take control.

Ares had a problem.

People would start asking questions when he didn't show up at the Pentagon, not to mention he was pulling a lot of strings to get more men. He'd reached out to a handful of former officers he had known years ago and asked them to start pulling together ex-military types.

The community was tight though and the word was spreading that these jobs had become a lot more dangerous, even if the money was good. Rumor was that a lot of men had died in Morocco on what was supposed to be an easy security job.

They'd already lost two dozen men and women who had just walked off the job after the prison incident. Said that taking on gods was not in the job description. The ones who had manned the first choke point had been talking and he couldn't get them to shut up. Not now. The rumor mill was at full strength in a tight knit community.

He sat in a cramped office and looked at The Colonel. Well, The Colonel in body at least.

"That halfwit Derek says they've been spotted in Egypt...says Zeus wants a team to go after them."

The Colonel kept fidgeting in his seat, stretching his neck and rolling his shoulders.

"They want us to clean up their mess."

Ares shared something with the man in his office that even the Titans didn't know about. They had both hidden it quite well and sold the lie to perfection. Ares had always been an angry sort of man that loved bloodshed. He had been a perfect match and was granted power in secret, away from the other Titans' watchful eyes.

The Titan war that had brought so many millions of souls, had been so invigorating, but the two had agreed that it wasn't for the best. The mortals would wipe themselves off the earth and the Titans would be left to start over. They craved souls for power, but they needed them in a slow, steady pace.

It was love they manipulated instead. Pretended that was where the power came from.

The one who had taken the Colonel's body remembered climbing that mountain and begging them to stop fighting. That they were bringing the end of the mortals to reality. That it had to stop.

Themis had been easy to convince, she did love her precious justice. She thought it was all her idea, but he had planted the seeds in her mind.

Ares had done his job well back then. He knew the other guards well enough to play to their deepest desires. Power. Status. Wealth. Control. Knowledge. He spoke the words to plant the corruption in their hearts and it had all gone much faster than any could have predicted.

Demeter knew where the hidden armory was and led them right to it. They stole the weapons and the Smith did what he could. Only one with knowledge of the Titanic powers could have passed the immortality on though. Even with the weapons they needed someone with that knowledge.

Only one of them had intimate knowledge of both life and death.

He flexed his hands and looked down at them. At the very least this new body was well built. The Colonel did take care of himself.

His old body had a structural problem, being that the throat had been cut and all. He hadn't liked taking over The Colonel and dragging his own body out like that. Passing himself as faded and weak had been hard enough but controlling two bodies was much harder than he had expected. Not to mention the ruining of his original form, it would take months to heal before he could take life in it again.

Iapetus had taken The Colonel for his own, but Ares' pet soldier was buried deep under a Titan mind. His mind screamed to be free, but it was useless.

"So, what do we do?" Ares asked his mentor. Iapetus had spent only a few years in his cell before the Olympians took power, with his help of course. He knew this world better than they did.

"Send a team to Egypt. I don't know why their pilot is taking them in the wrong direction, they must know where Zeus is by now. He must have a plan of some kind, maybe skirting the facility or finding a way to throw us off their trail. Hyperion will go for Zeus, I'd bet on it."

Ares nodded, picked up his phone and dialed an old friend.

"Sam, yeah, it's me. I need some of your guys on a plane. Yesterday would have been good but I'll take two hours. Good. Thanks."

He set the phone down and watched Iapetus fidget in the Colonel's body.

"It's not that bad," he offered.

Iapetus rolled his eyes. Then settled into the chair and thought aloud.

"Shouldn't have ever let them all out, that was a mistake. A costly one. I assumed Zeus had prepared enough to stop them all. The chain was an oversight. He never told anyone about that. All these years of searching everywhere but there. Why would we ever look there?"

"It's too late now," Ares said. "We have other things we can deal with."

Iapetus nodded, flexing his new hands out again.

"Yes. We must find the others. And quickly."

Ares dropped a stack of brown files on his desk, each marked with a name in black ink. There were eight files worth of names and a small picture clipped to each. He fished out one file and opened it.

They had been watching her ever since the falling out.

"We know where she is, she might know where some of the others are."

Iapetus picked up the file with the only clear photo. She wasn't hiding like the others were. He couldn't help but admire that. Brave.

"Let's go talk to her then."

He threw the file back on the desk. Her profile was there.

She had become a Dean of a prestigious university, spoke dozens of languages and had firmly been against any involvement in Tartarus.

She went by a different name in the mortal world, but the file listed her true name.

Aphrodite.

Chapter XVI

Singapore is a bustling port city of an amazing scale and size. We gather and stand on the deck of the ship, watching other massive vessels come and go. Our own ship cruises in under the deft guidance of an experienced crew. Of course, there was some assistance from Oceanus. I don't think I've ever seen him so happy to be back on his beloved ocean.

The city stretches to the sky with its buildings and it is beautiful.

I almost regret having to come for such a violent reason.

When the ship docks we disembark with blessings from the crew. Oceanus promises them steady seas for as long as they sail, and the men laugh it off. Sounds crazy to them, it would sound crazy to anyone after this long. Gods aren't real after all.

They are good enough types, having taken us on board like that and they will have his gratitude. Though they may never truly know it.

We stand on the dock surrounded by workers and the bustle of a busy port, sort of lost. Unsure of ourselves. Ten Titans in a brand new mortal world trying to track down a stolen weapon and a half god.

"So, where to?"

Jeff looks surprised to be asked.

"What? I don't know, I've never been here before."

Excellent. That hadn't occurred to me, not even once.

Mnemosyne points up at a building that overlooks the port with a very large symbol emblazoned on the top of it.

"Probably there."

She was more than likely right. The logo was a trident surrounded by lines that I suppose were meant to be waves. There was a single letter, angled almost as if the mast of a sailing ship. It was a very ostentatious and large letter 'P'.

Yeah. That was probably it.

Poseidon stood from his desk and walked to the window, watching the ships come and go. He opened a door to an expansive balcony and lit a cigar, walked to the railing and leaned on it, blowing smoke out into the open air and taking in the air that smelled of salt and oil and ships and industry. He loved that smell when it mingled with the cigar.

He knocked a chunk of ash from the cigar and looked down, thinking about his new plan. If the Titans didn't kill Zeus they would take losses, that was certain. Fewer Titans for him to deal with. Maybe they would go after Ares when they had killed Zeus and leave him just a few to mop up. Demeter was fiery, but she was all about self-preservation. Dionysus would come back to the fold once there was safety. The coward. Hera…well Hera would follow Zeus right to the bitter end. She would have to die too.

He knocked the cigar again and smiled, it was a good plan. Hyperion would have his revenge and Poseidon would rise from the ashes-

He stopped thinking. Just stared down to a plaza where a group stood, one of them pointing at his building.

He knew them.

He dropped the cigar and sprinted for his office, picked up his phone and punched in the number.

"Get the helicopter here, now!" he shouted to his protege while he waited for Zeus to answer the phone.

"They're here!" he shouted into the phone. "They're outside my fucking office!"

"Was that…"

"Yup."

Oceanus stretched his head to the left, then to the right. Held his right arm across his torso and then the left, bent down and touched his toes, then raised his arms to the sky.

"What are you doing?" I say, watching him with a raised eyebrow.

"You should always stretch before any strenuous physical activity brother; did you learn nothing in the pit?"

I snort at him.

"Jeff, you can go find somewhere to wait this out if you'd like. Phoebe, take Coeus and go with him.

She agreeably took Coeus' arm and the three of them left the plaza. Coeus was currently a liability for us, one more to protect.

We could see the lobby from where we stood and perhaps it hadn't been smart to get so close, but it was too late now. You can't go back, you can only go forward. People filed out of the building as alarms rang out in the calm afternoon sun, heading for local coffee shops to wait it out.

I lifted my head to the sun and felt the warmth soak into my face, drinking in the rays and letting the power run to my fingertips.

"If we do this, we can't go back." Kronos speaks the words, but he knows the answer. We all know the answer. Titans are not to be forgotten.

We are gods. The mortals will remember this.

Poseidon may not have been expecting us, but he doesn't lack in security. At least eighteen of them pour from the building in full tactical equipment, rifles held up at the ready. They form a loose semi-circle a reasonable distance away while people scream and run from the scene. It takes maybe thirty seconds for the plaza to be emptied with only a ring of civilians watching and holding up their phones.

"Don't move!" one of the men shouts, his voice distant over the gap.

"Have you thought this through?" Kronos shouts it, opening his hands to the sky and stepping past me. "Do you really want to do this?"

"I said don't fucking move!"

Kronos looks to me and nods.

I smile.

Fire swirls around my hands, slowly building into an inferno that courses around my body. The heat and fire buoy me and I rise on a flaming pillar that grows higher and higher into the air. The heat doesn't faze me, but I can see people wincing and recoiling from it. The men step back, mouths open as they watch, rifle barrels dropping as they lose their focus.

"Drop your weapons now or taste the wrath of a Titan! I am Hyperion, lord of the sun and sky, ruler of flame and death, bringer of the end! Will you face me, or will you kneel?"

I shout it out through the flames, feeling a little silly about the overboard dramatization of it all but...well mortals do love theatrics.

The guards look nervous, casting glances to the speaker who had so rudely ordered us to not move. He looks at me and I see the decision being made. The wrong one.

"Open fire!"

He is first to raise his rifle and begin shooting, so I bring up a shield of flame that melts the bullets. The others begin shooting as well, pelting the column with their bullets. I feel the fire slipping in strength as the bullets seep into my power, they are forged from the armory and sap my strength even if they do not strike me.

That is why I didn't come alone.

The shooting stops, quite suddenly, and I see through the swirling flame. Tethys easily tosses one of the men to her elemental. Kronos punches one across the face and it almost hurts me, I remember that impact even after all these years. Themis lifts yet another above her head and tosses him into two more, bowling them over. Mnemosyne leaps through the air and strikes a man in the face with her knee and I hear bones breaking even through the firestorm. I think it was the one who demanded we not move though I'm not sure I could recognize him now.

I'm not sure anyone could.

When Rhea summons her lion forth from the ground the fight ends.

I've always found it amusing in a way. A column of fire or the control of the sea or even Kronos' gift of the earth bending to his will are not enough to send fear through a mortal heart. It's always Rhea and her lion that do it, that molten rock beast is the line for a mortal.

The rest of the men quickly throw down their weapons and drop to their knees, holding their hands above their heads. The crowd around is silent, no screaming or running as they hold up their phones still and talk excitedly among themselves.

These mortals are much different than I remember. Less fearful.

I allow the flame to dissipate and drop to the scorched stone of the plaza but there is little time to deal with the mortal crowd before we are distracted.

As we stand there we hear a thumping sound that sounds quite familiar. An aircraft appears over the city skyline and approaches the building. It's still a long way off but it's gaining on the building.

An escape.

We see a figure on the balcony, still looking down at us but now holding a golden trident.

Oceanus looked up as well and I don't think I've ever heard him get so loud. That's saying something.

"I'm going to kill you!"

Then he was off, sprinting into the building's lobby without a moment of thought while the rest of us tried desperately to catch up.

Kronos and I were the last into the building.

"I suppose they know about us now."

I look back to the crowd with the phones up, most still unsure of what they had just seen.

"You might be right."

As we cluster in the lobby there is a deafening roar of gunfire from above that sends all of us scattering for safety as bullets thump into the many decorations and walls of the lobby.

Oceanus looks positively chastised, which is good because that was what we were going to do.

"Ah." He says, grinning, "my bad."

The guards that were busy shooting at us were holding a second level overlooking the lobby and there were a lot of them. Either they had been expecting us or Zeus was walled in behind even more security. Either option wasn't appealing.

I duck as chips of stone hit my face from the bullet impacts, cursing the armory under my breath.

If we hadn't stocked it so well, we wouldn't be here.

A bullet grazes my forearm and I flinch, looking down as thick blood seeps out and a small ring of black veins spread away from the wound. Direct hits would be much worse.

I launch a small burst of fire, but it goes wide and high, hitting harmlessly well above their heads. There's too many and they have the high ground along a walkway perched on several stone pillars that rings the building lobby. Two curving staircases lead upwards but charging up would be certain death. A wide reception desk of marble and stone is our hiding place, bullets hammering away as they shoot down.

When it stops for a moment none of us is willing to hazard a look. Then the floor shakes, as if something very heavy had landed on it.

"Hyperion!" a voice shouts, "come out and die."

Kronos shakes his head at me, mouthing something about a trap.

Maybe.

I think I'll take those odds. Better than dying like a cornered rat.

I stand, bracing for the hail of bullets but it doesn't come. Instead I see him.

The floor is caved in slightly under his armored feet. He looks eight feet tall but much of that is the armor he's wearing. It's a humanoid framework that supports his body and makes him much larger. He punches into one of the concrete columns and it explodes under the impact, sending shards through the lobby.

Gives him strength too, apparently.

"Come then!" he has a wild look in his eyes, stepping towards me like he expects to win this fight.

I don't move as he closes the distance. As he raises an armored hand to strike. I don't need to.

We're not so stupid as to fight alone. Not anymore. Not like him.

He's too busy closing the gap to see the water that slithers along the floor, winding its way up a leg and through the framework until it reaches his head. He's too busy until he's not.

If I hadn't been so close I might have missed it.

The water plugs his nostrils and mouth and he slowly comes to a stop, a few feet from his goal. As his breathing is stopped the crazed look fades from his eyes and is replaced with panic. He tries to gasp a breath, I can see the movement in his mouth and throat and chest, but no air comes. He tries again. He unstraps an arm from the suit and claws at his face, slowly turning blue.

He drops to his knees and shatters some tiles. His eyes roll back in his head and he falls forward with a *thump*. The water slips away from his face while the rest of the men on the upper landing stare down.

Their hero.

Their titan.

"Open fire!" one of them yells but they are too slow. Their idiot broke one pillar. That leaves three and I am close enough now. I swing wide and long, letting the chain carry itself out and through the three pillars. One by one it cuts through them with an explosion of dust and shards, one by one they are no more.

The upper landing shudders.

The men run but not fast enough, with all their weight and without the support it starts to tip. Then it comes crashing down.

They skid down the length, some falling the fifteen feet or so to the hard floor below as the landing crumbles around them, others caught in the tumbling cascade of crumbled metal and stone. They stumble to their feet and to their credit, or stupidity, they don't give up and go for their weapons.

"Hyperion, Oceanus, go!" Kronos pushes us towards a door marked with an image of stairs, "we'll take care of this. You two go get him."

Kronos charges off into two of the guards as they rise, tossing them aside like rag dolls while more come towards the building from outside, including one more wearing a heavy suit. Where are they getting all these mortal fools from?

Kronos and the others can handle it, so we go to the stairs and we start upward. A long climb to where another god waits, perhaps calmly, for our arrival.

A lesser god.

Sort of.

This will be interesting.

"Shit, shit, shit." Poseidon rushed through his office, stopping only briefly to feel the power of the trident in his hands. It is unfamiliar, the thing had become more of a decoration to him than a weapon. His hands don't remember the weight or the feel, it's unbalanced and awkward.

"Shit! Where is the chopper?"

His protégé looks up, hands shaking and nerves failing.

"Five minutes sir. We should go to the roof."

"No fucking shit!" Poseidon yells, going for his office door. Yanking it open he sees two men running down the hall and slams it shut again.

"Shit!"

The door opens briefly, and we see him. Then the door slams shut, like he hoped we didn't see him.

Like a flimsy door will stop us.

Oceanus takes the lead and throws his beefy shoulder into the door and it explodes off the hinges, flying inward before being split in half by a trident. The pieces fall harmlessly, and Poseidon stands there. He is fatter than I remember but the crazed look in his eyes doesn't bode well.

Another man takes shelter in the corner of the office, covering his head and screaming.

"Come on then!" Poseidon shouts, coming forward with a thrust of the trident.

We dodge it easily as the trident moves between us, but he jerks it to the side and sends Oceanus through the air into a bookshelf with a heavy thud. Books tumble to the floor and Oceanus shakes his head as he stands. I see the marks of blood soaking into his shirt, the trident is powerful.

The trident comes back towards me, so I drop under it, sliding on the floor for a few feet and lashing out with the chain. He sidesteps it and the chain shatters one of the windows overlooking the docks, shards of glass tumbling into the open air.

A closed fist hits me in the side of the face and I see stars as my head snaps to the side into his heavy wooden desk. He stands over me with the trident, prongs down and raised high before a blur of motion hits him around the midsection and both he and Oceanus tumble across the office.

I manage to stand just as a shot rings out and a model ship shatters. I drop to a knee and spin, sending the chain out in a wide arc to hit the man that was cowering in the side of his torso. I hear ribs crack and he grunts, tumbling over the desk before coming to a stop on the floor and not moving.

Poseidon stands as Oceanus is distracted for a moment by the shot, sending the bottom of the trident handle into my brother's chin with a loud *crack* and he falls backwards, clutching his jaw. When he recovers there is blood seeping between his teeth and one is missing.

I have no time before Poseidon throws another model ship at me and I duck under the heavy glass case.

When I recover Poseidon is gone from the room.

"No!" I pull Oceanus to his feet as he shouts it, as we both hear that growing thumping and see a helicopter closing the final distance on the rooftop.

There's no time but we run anyway.

He can't get away.

He just can't.

The helicopter hovers over the rooftop just as we come out through one of the access stairwells, running in a dead sprint as it comes lower and lower towards Poseidon.

It's too far and the helicopter is too low. We're going to lose him. From the door of the helicopter a man raises his rifle towards us.

Gunfire erupts and both Oceanus and I hit the concrete, but bullets don't hit us, or even near us. Instead the distinct noise of metal on metal shrieks above the thumping of the helicopter as sparks flash along its body.

"Get him!" our newly arrived support shouts, walking calmly towards the helicopter and reloading before firing again. One of the bullets hits Poseidon in the shoulder and he drops the trident as his body experiences mechanical failure. The man in the helicopter tries to shoot again but Jeff fires the rest of his ammunition into the man's chest and he tumbles out of the helicopter towards the very distant ground below.

The helicopter veers away under the hailstorm and Jeff looks at the two of us sprawled on the roof.

"Go!"

We pull ourselves up just as Poseidon hits Jeff with his good shoulder, as he charges towards the other door. Jeff slides across the roof with a grunt and his rifle disappears over the roof. We give chase as Jeff comes to a stop, turning over in obvious pain and using his pistol. He fires at Poseidon just as he disappears around the corner of the doorway.

As he did, two guards came around with their rifles up. They ducked back as Jeff continued shooting from his position on the ground.

Oceanus snatches up the trident and looks to me.

"Go!" I yell at him, "I've got this." He disappears towards the other stairwell and gives chase.

Jeff empties his weapon and rolls onto his back, his breathing doesn't sound right. There's no time for that.

With a few long strides I cover the gap to the door just as a guard steps out, his eyes open wide as I hit him, tackling him back into the concrete wall. The other comes forward, letting his rifle fall to the side and trying to drop a knife into my back. I elbow him in the gut and slam his head into the metal railing of the stairs.

He moans as consciousness becomes elusive.

From below I hear shouting.

"Kill them, kill them!" It's Poseidon and his voice cracks as he repeats the command. I laugh.

The man with the serious head wound has several round objects on his vest. He must be special to be entrusted with those. We'd had a crash course in the equipment from Jeff.

They were grenades.

I pull the "pin" out and hold it over the stairs. There's men rushing up.

I open my hand and let it drop.

The stairwell shakes as it explodes in the confined space, my ears ringing with the noise reverberating off the walls. I look down.

There are no more men rushing up.

The one I tackled tries to get to his feet, swinging his knife wildly at my legs. I grab his vest and lift him up, walking back on the roof where Jeff is on his feet now, clutching his chest.

"What are you doing?"

He asks.

I lean over the edge to look at the front of the building.

"You'll see."

Chapter XVII

Poseidon fled from the building, limping on his one good leg and clutching his shoulder as gunfire sounded in the office building he was leaving behind. He hadn't even had time to grab his phone to tell Zeus or Ares about it, there still wasn't time. He'd caught a bullet in his leg from that fool on the roof, armed with the Titanic ammunition. He limped his way towards his personal car that was pulling around to the front of the building.

Plan B.

It exploded outward under the impact of a heavy object being thrown from the higher levels of the building, the windows bursting and the roof crumpling inward. It was a man, or what was left of a man, dressed in tactical gear. One of the security team.

Poseidon looked up to see Hyperion staring down from the upper levels. Hyperion waved. Poseidon turned and ran as fast as he could on the injured leg, running for a long dock that would lead him to his prized personal boat. It was a long run on one good leg.

His ship was the Goddess of the Sea, of course.

He had lost his trident, but he could still escape. Zeus could help.

He ran down the length of the dock and stumbled onto his boat. He fumbled with the keys before the engine roared to life and he eased out into open water.

He looked back to see the nearest Titan wasn't yet close enough to stop him.

He turned back to the ocean and smiled. He had escaped.

It took him a moment to realize that the ocean was getting higher around him, not with waves but higher. The boat was driving down a ramp of sorts. Only a few seconds later the hull ground against the ocean floor and his escape was thwarted.

Surrounded by the walls of the ocean in a very nice cylinder, Poseidon looked around at his defeat. He had lost control of the ocean.

"Shit."

"It's only going to get worse..."

The voice startled him but the impact of the trident handle on his jaw was worse, sending him spinning to the floor of the boat with a grunt. Then he was picked up by strong arms and heaved onto the ocean floor with an earth-shaking thud. He raised his head just in time to take the handle of the trident again to the bridge of his nose.

His nose exploded, and he clutched at his bloody face, struggling to his knees despite the pain.

"You stole everything!" Oceanus roared, lifting Poseidon up and slamming him down into the ocean floor again. This time Poseidon didn't get up, he just lay there gasping for air.

"You took everything from us first." Poseidon finally managed.

Oceanus knelt beside his former friend and looked him in the eyes.

"We paid for that. You went too far. Made yourself into a god."

Poseidon's eyes went from fearful to defiant with a flash of rage.

"I am a god!" he shouted through broken teeth and seeping blood.

Oceanus gripped the trident tight and stood, walking toward the wall of seawater that rushed around the two. He stood at the wall for a moment and then looked back. He thrust the trident into the boat and tore a gaping hole, she would take on water and stay forever buried in the waves.

"You were a pretender. The sea shall take you."

He stepped into the wall and the sea carried him safely away.

Poseidon shouted at the sky, the water, everything he could. In rage, defiance, then begging. He held up his hands against the seawater, but it did not yield. It was not his. Not anymore.

The water gripped him tight and as the walls crashed into the boat and the ocean reclaimed all that was hers. Poseidon was dragged towards open water with a mighty current. He clawed at the dry ocean floor even as water crushed his hands and filled his lungs and the screaming faded.

Then he was gone.

The ocean belonged to her master once again, carrying Oceanus to safety on a strong current.

Oceanus stood on the beach with the other Titans that had come from the tower, he had been faster, and it was his place to choose the fate of Poseidon. He clutched the trident and stared over the calm ocean.

"He was my friend."

Kronos stepped forward and put a hand on his brother's shoulder. He was the first of us to kill one of them. I suppose it hadn't really sunk in that we'd be killing our former friends. Even with the betrayal of our trust they had still meant something at some point.

Oceanus sighed, wiping his eyes and held up the trident.

"Does anyone know a good smith?"

Chapter XVIII

The Smith often wondered about the use of "crucible" as a place to test one's ability to overcome. It, famously, was a place of destruction. Everything after was where the rebuilding came, where the molten metal would become something of use. A tool.

Perhaps that was it, he mused. You must be destroyed before you can become what you were meant to be. That might make sense.

Still silly. He was the one who chose what the molten metal became in the end, that implies a force may choose what comes from the crucible. Is that what they mean? He wiped the beaded sweat from his forehead with a thick, hairy forearm and wondered just how grimy he must look. His thick beard was tangled with sweat and dirt and the stink of the forge.

With the prison open he knew that it was a matter of time. Someone would win this skirmish but that was all this was. A handful of petulant "gods" against true gods. He had an inkling of who would win but who could ever be certain. He had wanted to help but there was something larger at work. Whether it was a cause, or an effect relationship was to be determined.

There were pantheons that had coexisted for a very long time, avoiding the conflict between the gods that had built one small city-state before turning to personal gain.

"Corrupt gods are not new," he said to himself, hammering away at an axe head for his current allies. He stopped and let the sweat drip down for a moment before shaking his head like a great shaggy dog. His focus was off.

"A craftsman should only have one thing on his mind," a thickly bearded man spoke, placing a heavy and calloused hand on The Smith's broad shoulder. This man appeared to be in his sixties but was built like a wrestler or warrior, muscled and tough. There were two others with him, one as impressively built and the other much slighter of build. The Smith looked down to the malleable light he had been working on shaping into just one more weapon of incredible power. They were god-killers.

"His craft," he said in reply, as was his way. He had been using that line for thousands of years and yet today he could not get the Titans out of his mind.

He wiped the returning sweat from his brow with a thick forearm and looked up to the group staring at him. A half dozen Cyclopes milled around the massive forge in the open expanse of the often-cold country they had taken refuge in. They were at least twice his height and thickly muscled, having worked forges their whole lives, but even so the Smith could give them a run in a contest of strength.

They could still drink him under the table.

"Poseidon is dead."

The man with the thick beard looked at The Smith with his one good eye, offering the good news up.

The Smith snorted, looking down at the arrows he had been crafting from the light. They would need them, perhaps soon. God-killers were vital when one was beginning a fight against gods. Fairly obvious really.

"One of them is there? It's the quick one, right?" The Smith said, leaving the light alone for a moment to focus on the conversation. It was no loss given that he had no focus on his craft.

The oldest and largest of the trio nodded, scratching under his beard.

"Yes, he'll help them now. Now that we've found them. We've chosen a side in this and it's only a matter of time before these Olympians find that out."

Hephaestus, known among the pantheons only as The Smith, went back to hammering. His focus was back, he had purpose with this light. As the group left he shouted after them.

"A war is coming, are you ready?"

The oldest one smiled before he stepped back into the night.

"We were born for war."

"Soldiers are superstitious," the Corporal said idly, wiping sand out of his receiver and blowing the loose bits away. "Goddamned desert."

He said the last under his breath. His Lieutenant grinned, none of the men were particularly fond of the granules of sand that seemed to work into their clothes and weapons and vehicles and all the way under their skin. They hated it.

"I'll take a bullet over another roll in the sand," the Warrant would often quip, even if that was a bold lie. The Lieutenant understood that bitching was the only way his soldiers could deal with this strange world. They had spent so much time in it now that it seemed more like home.

Hermes quietly cleaned his own weapon and laughed along with the troops as they cracked rude jokes and poked fun of the daily punching bag, whoever it happened to be that day. He had gained a reputation as a formidable soldier with an astonishing level of insight, luck, whatever they wanted to call it.

He was a broad-shouldered man that moved with surprising ease. In basic training he had been chosen to carry the SAW, a weighty weapon and all the ammunition that went with it. His instructors had meant it as a challenge, to slow him down because not one of them could outrun him in either distance or speed. They had been impressed but in basic there was no impressed and that had turned into countless push-ups and planks as punishment.

Years later he was a rising star that seemed too humble to continue up the ranks, rather comfortable with being where he was. None of the others complained about it, his seemingly sixth sense about things and astounding speed were their good luck charm.

Hence superstition.

They were on their sixth day of uneventful patrol and they had become bored. When the first crack of enemy gunfire sounded out there was a half second of pause before the controlled chaos erupted, as it always did. The perimeter sentries opened fire in return, hitting the sand and firing from prone. Vehicle gunners joined the foray and in moments the air was filled with bullets.

The Lieutenant was directing the firefight when an enormous weight struck him around the waist and he was thrown to the ground just as the *crack* of a bullet snapped right where his head had been before harmlessly sinking into the sand beyond. The Lieutenant didn't have a chance to say anything before Hermes was off to another place. The Corporal held out his hand and pulled the Lieutenant up and they both took cover behind one of the vehicles before it happened again.

As the Lieutenant slowed his breathing to get his racing heart under control he looked at the Corporal who just shrugged.

"Superstitious, sir," he watched Hermes pull another man out of the line of fire and then shoot back at the unseen assailants with precision. "Doesn't always mean it's wrong. Believe in something, out here whatever keeps you alive is best."

Months later, after returning home, Hermes was on a training exercise with a group he was proud to call friends. The roar of prop engines thundered in the sky, drowning out any pretense of conversation. Two rows of men in camouflage uniforms lined the riveted metal floor, wearing heavy backpacks and carrying rifles. They waited for the order to move forward and take the leap into the night.

Hermes stood in his place in line when he felt a vibration in his tactical vest. He fished his phone out to check the text message. It was an unknown number to his phone but not to him. It only had two words and it made his heart stop.

Titans Out.

He replaced the phone in his vest and waited, hands shaking. One of the soldiers noticed and flashed the thumbs up, which Hermes returned with the cockiest grin he could muster under the circumstances. When they piled out of the plane, there was one less parachute open than they expected. When the soldiers gathered at their training point under the cover of darkness they found their head count to be one short.

In the distance a pair of boots hit the ground, ditching the parachute he'd opened far away from the others. He sprinted away, dodging trees and breathing evenly, though his heart pounded wildly. He ran into the darkness. As the others began to search for him, Hermes disappeared into the night.

Chapter XIX

Zeus slumped into his chair for but a moment before he stood and threw the phone across his office in a fit of rage. It exploded on the wall and Derek flinched as shattered plastic and glass fragments hit him.

"Damn it!"

He pounded his desk with heavy hands and a crack sounded out in the office as the desk gave out slightly under the hit.

"Damn it! I was too certain they would come for me."

Derek flinched and stepped back from the desk. Zeus took a few heaving breaths to calm himself, allowing him to think clearly. They should have stayed close together. It had been a mistake to separate but it was too late for that now. Poseidon was dead. The trident was gone.

This had gone poorly. Not to mention security personnel were ready to riot when they heard the news that more than twenty had died protecting a shipping magnate. They had come on for easy protection work, nothing like this. That, plus the damned video of Hyperion playing on nearly every screen in the country was not good.

So far, the leading theory that had picked up traction was it was a movie set or something along those lines but that was rapidly falling apart as the body count started to rise. Money buys only so much silence. Now the talking heads were just spitting theories from superhumans to a fake video and that didn't include the conspiracy nuts.

Some of them weren't all that far off.

At least there was one upside.

They were quickly being left with the security personnel that had taken the job for one reason.

To kill.

"What now?" Derek said quietly, looking to his boss.

Zeus pinched the bridge of his nose and tried to drive away the headache building behind his eyes over this whole fiasco.

"I don't know."

Ares and Iapetus arrived on the campus just as the news was breaking about Singapore, where a man had summoned a pillar of fire and at least twenty men were being reported as dead. Ares was sure that would mean more men would be quitting the security teams, they were humans after all. No one was dumb enough to stay on a job with the odds of death rising higher, despite a sizable paycheck.

He turned off his phone, putting the problem out of his mind for the time being, while Iapetus led the way to the office of the Dean, where they would find her.

"How can I help you?" the young man behind the desk was friendly and his voice had a pleasant lilt, offering a smile as they entered. "Do you have a meeting?"

"No, but she'll be seeing us," Iapetus walked to the door with a name he didn't know and pushed it open to see her behind the desk.

Seated at the desk was a woman that looked to be in her late forties or early fifties, slim build and wearing a loose blouse with a black jacket. She did not look impressed to be interrupted until she saw Ares, then her shoulders sagged, and she waved off the young man. She stood and walked to the door, ushering them in and looking to the young man.

"It's okay, hold my calls."

She closed the door and turned her attention to the gods in her office.

She crossed her arms and looked at them over her thin rimmed glasses, adopting a severe look. Iapetus had always admired her attitude, it was much livelier than the others like her. Not a Titan but not an Olympian, something in between.

"What the hell do you want? Come to kill me, finally?"

"I wish." Ares shrugged. "What? Would be easier."

"Shut up," Iapetus chided the man and Aphrodite looked from one to the other, then it dawned on her. She started to laugh, making her way back behind the desk.

"Iapetus, you've changed haven't you. Taking his little bulldog is a nice touch. Can I expect this to be a permanent change?"

"It's temporary but I do appreciate your concern."

She barked a rueful laugh, taking her glasses off and setting them on the desk. Iapetus had always liked her, maybe too much for his own good. Killing her would have been easier but now he was grateful they hadn't. She might be able to help.

"What do you want?" she said, getting them to business. "Why are you in my office? We had an agreement."

"You've heard, I assume?" Iapetus still wasn't used to this body and shifted uneasily in the chair.

"That the Titans are out? No, I hadn't. It hasn't been all over the news or anything. I haven't seen Hyperion's face plastered in every Tweet for the past twenty-four hours. You know, I told you so. Always wanted to be able to say that to all of you. If you wanted to survive out here, you should have just left well enough alone. But no, Zeus wanted more. He always wants more."

"Where are the others?"

She leaned back in the chair and raised an eyebrow.

"I'm sure I don't know what you're talking about."

"Where are they? We need to talk to them."

She laughed again.

"Talk to them? Even if I did know where they were I would never tell you. They don't want to be part of any of this. I honor my agreements and promises, unlike others."

Ares lurched out of his chair and slammed his hands on her desk, leaning forward. She didn't move a muscle. He pointed a thick finger at her and opened his mouth to shout some threat, surely, except he didn't get a chance to speak.

She grabbed that finger and twisted it, the snap of bone echoing in her office as she leaped over her desk. Both tumbled back into the chair as Ares opened his mouth to scream or maybe to say something, but the tip of the knife dug into the flesh under his chin as Aphrodite kept a knee in his groin and pushed down.

He whimpered.

"Big man," she whispered, pushing the point of the blade until blood welled around it. "Try something now."

"Enough!" Iapetus stood from his chair so fast it fell backward, he stopped as the door opened and the young man with the friendly tone leveled a shotgun at his chest. She had been the one to secret the Smith out of Zeus' compound, they would have the right weaponry.

"Quite," the young man said, smiling politely.

Iapetus snorted, raising his hands as Aphrodite stepped back from Ares and he rubbed at the blood dribbling from his chin.

"Get out." She said, running her hands over her now creased pants and blouse, straightening them out. "Now."

They obliged, slowly.

"We'll find them," Iapetus said it as they left her office. "With or without you. Then we'll be back."

He shut the door.

The young man lowered the shotgun from his shoulder and breathed out, looking to her.

"That was fun."

She shook her head at the young man, the hidden progeny of one of the Titans that she had spirited away before the Olympians took power. He had been with her ever since, just another one of the many scattered Titanic children. That didn't include the Olympian children, none of them could keep it under control.

Like rabbits, she mused, yet they had distorted the myth to make her the one that couldn't bother to keep it in her pants.

"Are the others in place?"

She sat behind the desk and gave herself a moment to mourn the woman she had become, who could now be no more. They would come for her if she stayed, she had gone too far this time. Ares would remember it.

"Yes, it's just a matter of time before they show up to knock on someone's door."

She nodded.

"They'll need help. Soon. I suppose it's time to take a side."

He snorted and rested the shotgun over his shoulder.

"I think we just did."

Chapter XX

Oceanus has his new trident, despite all the grumbling about it. I have my chain. Even with both of those we have a long way to go.

Not to mention that, as a group, we were famous. Or I was. The guy in the flames does make an impression. We were becoming the most wanted and the most watched, at the same time. I was informed that this is an impressive feat.

Jeff had found a building under construction with a watchman that might have been as old as us. It was as good a place as any to work out a plan. He was wincing with every step but waved the concern off.

Tough, I like it.

"They'll be coming for us now," Kronos said. "We need to split up."

"That's stupid." I heard it come from my own mouth and slammed it shut. Not fast enough though.

"Go on." Kronos was glaring. Can't really blame him.

"We're stronger together, we should keep it that way."

"He's right," Phoebe spoke up, and I offered her a smile of gratitude.

"No not you…" I stop smiling. "…Kronos is right. Coeus can't fight, we need to find someplace safe where I can try to help him, not being dragged across the world where we'll slow you down. As a group we're too big, too much of a target."

I suppose she was right.

"So, who goes where? What's our next move?"

I don't think anyone has an answer for that. This is a new world for all of us, not at all like the one that we left behind all those years ago. This is one city, one impressive city, and it's overwhelming. Where the hell do we go from here?

"I'm going after her." Kronos says it quietly, but it is heard, there is an edge to his voice I haven't ever heard before. Not even when we fought. Rhea stands by her brother, obviously.

Oceanus puts his hand on Tethys' shoulder and squeezes, moving past her to stand with the three.

"You'll need someone with a real damned weapon. Even if it's a fork. Not to mention all that ocean you'll be crossing."

"If you're going that way you'll need someone to keep you on the right path," Crius is next to join their group, "he's good with speed but direction…not so much."

"I can take them," Jeff steps up and motions to Phoebe and Coeus, "they'll be too busy tracking you all to realize we've split off. I can take them somewhere safe, maybe we can figure out how to help Coeus. I also think I've broken a few ribs, I could use a break."

Coeus stares off into nothing without even acknowledging his name.

"Thank you." Kronos speaks for all of us. Jeff blushes a little. Mortals. So emotional.

"If you're going after her then we'll go find Dionysus. If we dismantle them piece by piece it will be easier than just going after the head of the snake, right?"

I feel their eyes on me, some smile like there's some inside joke that I'm not a part of.

"What?"

"You have changed, we should have thrown you in Tartarus ages ago."

They laugh.

I don't.

"How do we get where we need to go?"

"I might be able to help."

The voice is not one of ours. It's someone else. And it comes from behind us. We all turn to see this person slowly stepping out with their hands held high in the air.

Tethys is gone before we can react, like a flash. She hurls herself at him and they both tumble to the ground. She doesn't summon her elemental. She doesn't need to. She's going to use her hands to kill him. She's going to choke the life from him with her bare hands and watch the light go out of his eyes.

She's making excellent progress on that and I don't move to stop it. I would do the same thing.

Before she does Oceanus grabs her arm, stopping her fist from slamming into his youthful face. Might knock some of those pretty teeth right out.

We gather around, and he looks up at the ceiling, closing his eyes and waiting for it.

"You've got about ten seconds before I let her go at you. Go."

He opens one eye to see Oceanus holding her arms pinned behind her back, though she's trying her best to break free of him.

"It's not what you think."

"Not a great start," I haul him up by his shoulders. "Do better."

"I'm sorry," he says it to Tethys, not the rest of us though, "I should have come back for you, a long time ago. I'm sorry."

She looks at him and her shoulders sag, the fight leaving her. Oceanus lets go of her arms, slowly. She takes a deep breath.

And she punches Hermes right across the mouth

Hermes rubs his jaw as blood leaks out through his teeth, teeth that might be a bit loose now.

"Good hit." I say.

It gets me a few glares. Tethys smiles a little, not much but a little. That makes it worth it.

Hermes struggles to his feet, shaking his head like that will help.

"How sorry can you be?" she screams at him when he's finally up. "You left us there!"

Hermes looks down to the floor and spits a gob of blood into the dust, rubbing it in with his boot.

"I know. I should have come before. I shouldn't have done it in the first place, really."

"So why now?"

Hermes looks up and the shame is gone from his eyes, replaced with anger. At least it looks like anger. Hermes was never one for that, but he has changed. I suppose we all have.

"Zeus told me what he wanted to do, and I wouldn't be part of it. Lots of us wouldn't. We lived with leaving you in there, but he wanted more, needed more."

"How did you even find us?" Themis asking the important questions, which was good since we apparently had a fountain of knowledge now.

"It was easy. We split up and one of us took one of them. Then we waited for things to blow up. Looks like I'm the lucky winner. Artemis owes me five bucks. I told her even with you…" he points at me, "…going for Zeus would be stupid."

"Thanks…I think?"

I'm not sure how to take that.

To save my own pride I'll take it as a compliment.

Tethys is still seething but Kronos steps in, distracting her.

"You said you could help us? How?"

Hermes smiled, still showing off some of that blood from Tethys' hit.

"You think they're the only ones that have resources?

"Why should we trust you?" Tethys almost spat the words, venomous. I love it. A river of rage, our little sister.

He reaches down and draws a dagger out from a sheath strapped to his ankle, holding it out palm up for Tethys.

"This belongs to you."

She takes it, running her fingers over the blade. It's hers alright, she moves like water with that thing. It's terrifying.

She looks at him, presses the tip of the blade into the flesh under his chin and flicks it, drawing blood and a wince from him.

"You'll be the first to die."

He nods, then steps aside for us to take the stairs back down to the main level.

I grab his shoulder and lean in close, might as well drive the point home. He looks nervous. Good.

"What she said."

Hermes leads us out of the building, a not so subtle group of Titans waiting for an ambush that doesn't come. He guides us through the streets and down to the docks, through a gated fence and into a rather large warehouse. He turns on a light to reveal a hangar and several storage crates lined along the sides.

At the end of the hangar is a door and as we crowd into the space a man steps out from it. He wears an open suit jacket and a red collared shirt, looking as cocky and arrogant as I remember. He walks across the gap towards us.

He looks at Hermes and the rapidly forming bruise that marks where Tethys' fist made contact. Then he looks to Crius.

"Let's not do that."

Crius surprises me, maybe all of us, by crossing the floor and embracing the man.

"I have missed you, you prick."

Then Crius punches him in the stomach, doubling the man over with gasping breaths.

"At least it wasn't the face," Crius says, reaching down and grabbing the coiffed hair and dragging him back to a standing position while the man grimaces and lets out throttled chuckles.

"Probably deserved that," he finally manages to say, straightening his suit jacket with a tug and smoothing his hair down. He's done well for himself in these years without us, he would though. He was always the sort to get his due no matter what, to find the coins buried in the mud.

"The bins are labelled for each of you. Some of us have done well enough, despite all this, and we want to help you now. You may not believe it but I'm among them. The helpers, that is."

Hades smiles as we open the containers with our names, staring down at the contents.

"Hurry up, we have lots of places to be and not that much time. Chop chop. Things to do and gods to kill."

Some imagine that the black market is a literal market with stalls stocked with all the various illegal needs that might strike the types who are interested in that sort of thing.

It's not so. It's a rather unassuming system of internet forums. One that the international intelligence and policing community had yet to crack was a very small gardening forum. It was well maintained but served a small community. That was likely how it had escaped notice for so long. The man who spent much of his time cruising the forums did provide gardening advice to those who stumbled on it accidentally. That probably helped.

He also sold a wide array of weapons and services tailored to the criminal community, the deep underground.

He had very few rules, though he was not without a conscience.

It had been difficult. He didn't want to sell weapons because that would hurt innocents, no matter who gave him their word. As one of them, he knew not to trust criminals.

He offered a different set of services. He became the concierge of the criminal underground. He brokered the connections and contacts and that gave him a feeling of being disconnected. He had the opportunity to be discerning when he found clients and years later he was one of the most powerful underground entities.

The man commanded a vast empire that operated under the noses of interested parties and countries. Including under the interested parties of his former associates that had gone through more legal but no less corrupt means.

Those same former associates were now gods of industry and had unknowingly even called upon him for assistance. He took some pride in that, those pricks thought they were so smart. Even so they had lost track of him.

They had tried to shove him into a dark corner and forget about him. They painted him as the unwanted stepchild of the gods, they had cast him out both in the constructed myth and in this mortal world. They had underestimated his ability to recover and his ability to be petty and vindictive.

It was without end, said ability.

He was petty and vindictive and damn it if he wouldn't bring them down, somehow. It wasn't until he received a message from a user he hadn't heard from in years. The prison had been opened.

He grinned ear to ear as he typed his reply. It was time to bring his resources to bear against his oldest foes. They had made a mistake by casting him down the way they had.

Hades had found an underworld and become a king in it.

"Now you look like Titans again, no more ill-fitting rags," Hades snaps one of Oceanus' suspenders and I grudgingly have to admit some gratitude towards him. No more worn out prison shoes or sailor discards. They aren't exactly the loose clothes I remember being all the rage when we were out but it's kind of nice. Form fitting but not restrictive. Fighting in style. Not to mention the documents he had provided for each of us.

"Passports, best forgeries in the world, they'll get you across any border," Hermes passes them out one by one. "Cash too. You need to start flying under the radar, if that's possible."

Not a bad point. The world has been without gods for a while, might be a surprise to them to find out they're real.

"Phones, paid for. We can chat at leisure," Hades hands those out, one by one. "And you have some things to learn now. The world is a whole new place."

"Why are you helping us?"

Themis brings a full stop to the movement in the hangar by asking it. It's a good question, a very good question. We can't know what will happen to the Olympians after all this, maybe without the weapons they'll just...die.

"Because what we did wasn't right, and this is how we make it right," Hades says it and I am surprised to not hear the usual arrogant tone from him, no snarky remarks. He's sincere about that.

Themis apparently feels the same way because she gives him a curt nod and that would appear to be the end of that.

"You want to split up I hear," and just like that, Hades is back, "probably for the best. Demeter is in Argentina and Dionysus is hiding out with some of his buddies in Russia. I can get you there, I'll even do it for free...this time. Then I'll take Phoebe, Coeus and your new friend here out of the way of the mess I'm pretty sure you're going to make. I think I know someone who might be able to help with that."

Jeff, likely nursing a few broken ribs, agrees to that. Phoebe won't leave Coeus' side so it's an easy choice, he needs to be out of the way.

"How are you going to do all that?"

Hades smiles and we follow him beyond the door he'd come through from, finding two sleek black jets waiting for us.

"Your new chariots await."

Oceanus looks at his trident and mutters something.

"What?" I say, turning to him and he frowns.

"I wanted to sail."

Chapter XXI

We didn't spend long on goodbye, who wants to when it might be the last goodbye?

Hermes offers to be our guide to Russia, something Tethys doesn't seem too pleased with but accepts. Mnemosyne and Themis are along for the ride as well, the four of us sitting in silence on the plane while we head to see about Dionysus.

He had styled himself as the god of wine, a stark contrast to the Dionysus that we all remember. Themis and Hermes sit together, and she pries information about Artemis out of him, Tethys sits and glares at Hermes while toying with her elemental. That just leaves Mnemosyne.

She's staring out the window. I assume she's thinking about her friend, at least he had been once upon a time. She can remember everything in perfect detail, probably playing through every conversation and every moment they had spent together and trying to remember something. Maybe a clue he was going to betray her. She just sits and stares.

I wonder how Theia would have felt about flying like this, being up in her clear sky. To be above the clouds like this and soar over the earth. She would have loved it.

I push the thoughts out of my mind and take the seat beside Mnemosyne. She looks over and goes back to staring.

"Do you think we should have seen it coming?" she asks me quietly, still staring out at the sky.

"I honestly don't know, maybe we were too distracted. Maybe they were too subtle."

She doesn't speak for a long time, just stares. Then she turns to me, cheeks wet with tears, and puts a hand on my leg.

"It's not your fault."

On my seat is the coiled black metal chain that holds my powers, that once split the clouds in the sky for the sun to come through and bring life to the earth. I look at it and wonder if I would have been able to resist the call of power if I had been Zeus. I should have known better than to trust him, to let him get close. We all should have.

I squeeze her hand before standing.

"Yeah, it is."

She goes back to staring and I leave to see Tethys, who won't stop glaring at Hermes.

"We should kill him," she says it through her teeth and the orb wiggles an approval of the suggestion.

"No, we shouldn't."

She tears her glare away from him and instead focuses it on me. The orb too.

"Could you forgive Zeus?"

I snort.

"Of course not, but you're better than me in most every way little sister."

"I'm older than you."

"Barely."

She elbows me in the side, a little harder than I'd like, but the glare softens. She's hurt but she is better than most of us, if anyone can forgive one of them it would be her. Maybe Crius, but he gets lost in the stars sometimes.

"I'll try."

"That's all we can do. Not like we're gods or anything..."

She elbows me again and then we laugh, killing the tension. I don't want to spend the flight thinking about Kronos and the others or what is waiting for us in Russia.

More death. Just like Phoebe said.

"Poseidon is dead."

Iapetus pinched the bridge of his nose for a moment before he kicked out and shoved a chair across the small office, shattering it against a bookcase. Ares waited for the Titan to calm himself, as he always did, before the next delivery of bad news.

"Aphrodite disappeared too, she slipped past my men."

"Isn't that just great!" Iapetus shouted, and a military officer poked his head in the door before quickly retreating when he saw the matchstick chair.

"What now?"

Iapetus took Ares' chair and sat down in it. They were losing men and they were bleeding Zeus' money. With Poseidon dead there would be a lengthy legal process before the funds became available. His protégé was dead too so they had just lost an enormous amount of their bankroll. Which they needed for the mortals. They did not help out of the kindness of their souls or fear.

They had found a silver lining though. The serious security personnel weren't leaving, the cocky ones that thought they could kill a god and the ones that cared more about the sizable increase in pay they would get for killing one. A bounty that Zeus offered.

"We were wrong, Hyperion apparently learned something over all those years. Maybe the others were just more convincing. I didn't think my brother would ever learn the meaning of nuance or restraint. We should consolidate now...wait."

Ares paused with his hand on the phone, staring at his mentor and master. More the latter than the former.

"I think I have an idea what they'll do next. And what we can do about it."

Kronos didn't speak much during his flight, instead opting to sit with Rhea in comfortable silence and think about Demeter. They had been more than friends, like some of the others, and she had betrayed him. It hurt.

Crius and Oceanus talked excitedly about the plane itself, Oceanus apparently having forgotten his desire to sail and Crius thrilled to be so close to the stars again. Hades was with Phoebe and Coeus, while Jeff slept in a seat. Sometimes he would wake and groan as he shifted, nursing at least a few broken ribs.

They were flying to Argentina with a brief stop for Jeff, Phoebe and Coeus. Hades had sent for Jeff's family. That had surprised Kronos. Hades had never seemed to be a caring type of person. Kronos had looked up what the Olympians had crafted as Hades' background only to find he was not a highly prized god among them. The master of the underworld that was disliked and cast aside.

Kronos wondered if that had hurt Hades, despite all the arrogance and bravado.

He ran his fingers over his lesser sickle, thinking back to Demeter. How she'd caught his eye. The mortals had spread across the earth at the time, the Titans spread out with them. Their first village had become a large city of thousands with small towns cropping up along the coastlines of the world as Oceanus and Crius guided ships across the vast oceans. She had been working a new field for the city and she was loud. She was ordering the others around as they removed stones and stumps, Kronos always felt that the mortals should be able to stand on their own and not rely on the power of a Titan. She had embodied that.

As the plow dug into the soft earth and created fresh furrows for seeding, she cheered with the rest. Kronos had fallen in love with her. Her strength and a love for the earth were too much for him to resist. Titans were not invulnerable to emotions after all.

Not long after that day, Hyperion started the war that had led them to Tartarus. Everything had changed since then.

Now she was corrupted. Something he wouldn't remember. Something he would have to kill. Maybe she had been corrupted from the beginning. Maybe he had made a mistake.

Either way, her betrayal stung him.

He thought about it for the length of the flight until they landed at a small airport in the darkness. Hades hurried the three that they would leave behind down the stairs to the tarmac where another group waited.

Kronos was getting tired of all the players on the board, it was getting hard to keep track.

Coeus blankly followed his sister to the group, who stepped into the light. Kronos recognized them through the plane window, most of them at least.

"Calm," Hades held up both hands, but it was useless. Everyone bolted past him and out of the plane after Jeff, Phoebe and Coeus.

One of the group on the tarmac stepped forward, looking ready to fight. Oceanus held the trident and Kronos his sickle as they both stared down the young man.

"Stop it, there's been enough violence over all of this!"

She stepped forward and spoke the commanding words, and she was the only one that Kronos didn't know. Two of the others were Olympians and the young man standing behind them was Iapetus' son.

A hero and champion of the mortals, the boy was well liked and always did what he thought was right for the mortals over the gods. Kronos had liked the boy before he had disappeared. As they fought their wars he vanished.

"Who are you?"

He rounded on this woman who felt she could command him and she placed a hand on his chest and he felt something in it. There was power.

Titanic power.

"But…how?"

She tilted her head at him.

"What, you think you were the only children they had? Titans may have come first but that doesn't mean you were the end. There are many gods. Lesser and greater."

Kronos couldn't believe it, it made sense of course but it was a lot to take in at once. Especially with the other two. Phoebe was too drained to be angry and Coeus was still not himself. Athena took his arm and looked in his eyes, those dead green eyes, and she started to cry.

"I'm so sorry."

Phoebe didn't look at her, instead, she rests her gaze on Apollo. He opens his mouth, but she shakes her head.

"Not now. Just. Not now."

The young man spoke for everyone after a long silence, an awkward silence as everyone seethed.

"Can this wait for another time? A better time?"

Kronos reluctantly agreed, pulling the others back towards the plane. Before they left he stopped Jeff, placing a hand on the mortal's shoulder.

"Thank you, for everything. We will not forget it."

At the top of the stairs, Kronos stopped and held out the sickle, pointing to the woman and young man, alternating between them.

"If anything happens to them, you die. You hear me, Prometheus?"

With that he was gone, leaving the threat lingering in the air.

Jeff wasn't surprised by these proclamations anymore, he just looked at the two and shrugged, idly rubbing his chest through the pain.

"He means it."

Chapter XXII

Demeter owned a vast area of property in Argentina, where she'd built a sprawling home to befit her status. It was filled with marble, statues and gaudy symbols of their former glory as the Greek gods, when they had lived in the public eye. When farmers came to pray in her temple and offer what little they had for the slightest favor.

They changed with the times, when the Romans became an imperial power she adapted, just like the others. Zeus had argued it, but she was smarter than he was, and she knew it.

They had grown fat and happy and content off the mortals until Zeus made a mess of it all. Now she would have to clean that up too. Maybe it was time for a new king of the gods, maybe time for a queen.

Now she walked her not so humble abode, pacing the floor and waiting. They had killed that fat fool Poseidon and she might be next on their list. They had sold her on this plan, Ares promising she would be completely safe. That they wouldn't expect it.

She remembered Kronos though and he wasn't stupid.

Her hope was that even if he wasn't stupid that he was blinded by her turning her back on him. Maybe he would slip up. Maybe he wouldn't gut her.

She ran her finger over the blade of his sickle, now hers, drawing a pinprick of blood from the blade. She watched it well up on the tip of her finger and felt comfort. Even if they made it to her she could hold her own.

Not like Poseidon. She hadn't forgotten the Titans, she hadn't bought her own myth. She had readied for the day they would open Tartarus.

She forged her myth on her own now, through blood and earth.

We land at a small, private airfield and I wonder how Themis will receive Artemis, being the one of us most unlikely to forgive a slight. Hermes knew she was waiting for us there and had told us in advance, maybe to keep the rage of the moment away. Maybe to buy some small favor from us.

Maybe just for fun. I don't know.

When I see Artemis standing at the base of the stairs it occurs to me that I won't have to wait very long to find out.

Themis slowly descended the stairs from the plane with plodding steps on the metal stairs that reverberate in the empty space.

Clang

Clang

Clang

It's delicious in the tension it creates. I stand at the top and lean, Tethys opposite me. Hermes quickly and lightly makes his way down the steps, envious grace for a rather large man, while Mnemosyne shakes her head at us. She judges what brings us amusement.

I shrug at her. To each their own.

Three thousand years with little entertainment, this is where I get mine. Themis is too set in justice to kill Artemis anyway. Probably punishment of some kind, just not death. She won't forgive what happened, but the only time Themis takes a life for justice is when a life has been taken. Such moral fortitude.

Themis reaches the floor and stares down Artemis for a long time, almost uncomfortably long. Artemis holds a bow in one hand and offers it up, horizontal, to Themis. Themis tears her glare away and looks the bow over, running her hands over the smooth surface and testing the weight of the bow before deftly flipping it and catching it again.

I applaud softly, and she gives me a look.

I stop. Clearly not the time.

Themis takes Artemis by the arm and they walk off together to a place where I am not. At least I assume that's where they go. Hermes summons us towards a separate room, perhaps to leave them alone or maybe to craft a great plan or course of action.

I say kick doors in and burn them all.

"I think we should go in hard and not give them a chance to dig in more."

Well he's not far from what I would have suggested, just in more words. I smile at him and he gives me a very strange look, withdraws a little. Worried perhaps. Maybe that I'll use him to break down the door? Or as a shield from their Titan weaponry?

Maybe he's a little worried about all of the above in their own ways.

"I am onboard with that." I do like simple plans. The less moving parts in a plan the less likely something will fail, that's just factual.

Mnemosyne rolls her eyes and I'd bet she thought I didn't see it. I did.

No one ever appreciates my tactical brilliance. Even if it wasn't my idea in the first place.

Hermes seems equally surprised by the agreement, as if he has forgotten who I am. I am the god of fire and sun and I do enjoy a fight. You either win and it feels like nothing can stop you or you die, and you've earned a good death. I always envied the Northmen and their approach to death. I wonder where they are. Probably enjoying their fabled afterlife.

Now is not the time.

"Where are they? Where are the doors we need to kick?" I say, to bring myself back to the moment at hand.

He rolls out a map and outlines where Dionysus is hiding out. Hiding out isn't an easy task if Artemis is tracking you, she was born for that. It likely hadn't taken her long to find her prey, even if he had gone to ground.

Themis returns and Artemis behind her.

"Worked it out?"

Themis nods and that's all we're going to get so I move on, not much point in trying to draw blood from that stone. Not a talkative Titan, our sister. Never was and that is not going to change now, even if I pester her with questions. It's time to focus on the task.

"So where is this place?"

Hermes shuffles uncomfortably, then sighs.

"Underground."

Perfect, the first place we all want to go back to. Who doesn't want to escape one underground prison just to walk into another? With more mortals looking to kill us though, so not entirely the same.

"Well?" I ask, looking to each of them.

They all nod in agreement and it is decided.

It's time to visit a drunk.

Chapter XXIII

Aphrodite and Prometheus took their wards to a small, quiet suburban neighborhood with unassuming homes. Athena sat in the backseat with Coeus, trying to get his attention but he simply stared ahead at the headrest of the seat in front of him and mumbled under his breath.

Phoebe stared out her window, ignoring Apollo. He didn't try to explain himself, he knew she had already heard it all before. Every possibility and every word he could have said. She had killed him in some, she had died in others, she knew every choice that could play out. Now it was up to her to decide which one she would live in. He knew that. So, he sat in silence.

It was all in all, most definitely, an awkward car ride.

Jeff sat wedged between Apollo and Phoebe, looking between them awkwardly and catching Prometheus' eyes in the rear-view mirror. Prometheus offered a sympathetic smile. Jeff ignored it.

They parked the car and piled out, Athena leading Coeus into the house with Phoebe and Apollo close behind. Jeff eased himself up the walkway to the door when a little girl with blonde hair appeared and he sped up, catching a blur of motion and lifting her up despite the pain shooting through his broken ribs. The other two weren't far behind and his wife urged them all back into the house while Aphrodite and Prometheus watched the street for any sign of life.

When there was no movement they disappeared into the house as well, a house that no one knew about, deep off their books.

It was safe, at least for now.

"You'll be safe here until we get back," Aphrodite waited for Jeff to finish his reunion before talking to him and Apollo. Phoebe wasn't leaving her brother and Coeus was being looked at by Athena, that left the two of them to watch over things.

"If anyone can help Coeus regain his mind, it's Athena." Prometheus offered but Jeff didn't seem impressed. He was well and truly sided with the Titans now and these…gods had hurt them. Badly.

"Where are you going?"

"We need help. They need help. We've got a few places to go that might turn up that help, but it will take a while."

Prometheus answered for Aphrodite and she didn't argue, they were his siblings after all. They were his responsibility to find, since he had hidden them away when things started turning towards a war.

"Don't be long," Jeff glanced through the front windows, "you're wrong if you think they won't find out about this place. It's a matter of time."

He still stood watching, even as the brake lights of their vehicle disappeared around the corner. His wife touched his arm and he placed a hand on hers.

"What have you gotten us into?" she asked him softly.

He could only muster a kiss for her forehead but no answer. He didn't have an answer.

"Do you believe in gods?" he said quietly after a long pause of staring into the darkness of the silent street.

She shook her head and he looked at her, very solemnly.

"I do."

A young woman held her head up high even as the blood flowed from the cuts on her forehead and from a broken nose, leaking between loose and completely shattered teeth. Ares had rolled up his sleeves for this one, letting Iapetus take a break. He stood over the young woman and absently rubbed at the pinprick point on his chin that Aphrodite had left him. Though the wound wasn't much it was his pride that had been cut deeply. He had taken it out on the young woman tied to the chair.

"Hestia, Hestia, Hestia, didn't think we'd find you?" Ares leaned forward and sank the tip of a knife into her knee. She screamed.

"Scream all you like, no one is coming for you." Ares said it, leaving the knife buried there.

Ares had never liked her, she'd been far too soft and overly concerned. She hadn't ever been convinced to betray the Titans. She had been forced to. They threatened to kill her, and she'd gone along with their plan in exchange for her life. She was weak.

Cowardice, he'd always thought. The others had given in to greed for power or other selfish desires. She'd given in so that she would live.

Ironic, seeing where she was now.

They'd found her in Greece, living as a nun and doing everything she could for the poor and destitute. How noble.

Ares twisted the blade in her knee and she screamed again. She and Aphrodite had been close, but Ares knew only one of them had any fortitude. One of them that gave him pause and one of them that made him nervous. It wasn't this one. It wasn't Hestia.

He removed the knife slowly, watching blood pool and run down her leg. She gritted what was left of her teeth and spat an enormous gob of tooth fragments and blood at his face with pinpoint accuracy. Ares fell back, rubbing his eye and shrieking while she laughed hysterically.

Ares snatched a bottle of water from a low table and emptied it over his eye before turning his attention back to her. Maybe she wasn't so weak after all.

"That's how you want to do it then," Ares growled at her, looking to the other woman in the room. She stood in the shadows, arms crossed over a white coat that was pulled tight. She carried a folded set of instruments that she was well versed in.

Hera stepped forward, unflinching at the emotions that would usually come from seeing what, essentially, was her sister.

Hestia was bloodied and beaten and tied to a chair. Iapetus sat reading in the opposite corner, not bothered by any of it. Indifferent and waiting for it to be over. He looked up at the bloodied Hestia and raised an eyebrow.

Hestia turned her chin up at him and smiled.

"That's how I want to do it."

Chapter XIV

Kronos and company had arrived in Argentina, with Hades acting as guide. As a group they were short on help, given that three of them had been betrayed. They did all know that Hades wasn't a loss to have on their team though, he was cunning. Sneaky, if one was feeling less gracious about what praise should be delivered to a clearly disliked "god".

At least, disliked by the Olympians.

As well as the Titans, perhaps with the sole exception of Crius.

Hades didn't seem to mind much, he took the sideways glances and general distrust easily. He was used to it.

"She's at her villa, not really bothering to hide. Either it's a trap or she's incredibly stupid. I'd guess after Hyperion's little show in Singapore, it's probably option A."

He grinned at the collective, who ignored his glibness in favor of the map he'd procured of her villa. It was a sprawling affair, the grounds well-kept and dotted with marble statues and a wide staircase leading up to Greco-Roman columns that framed the massive house. It was perched on the top of a hill and the grounds offered line of sight for at least a mile in any direction for any patrolling guards or sentries.

"There's not really another option," Oceanus rubbed the chip in his trident and looked over the map, "even if we wait until nightfall we'll be spotted before we get near her. If she's even in there."

Hades adopted an offended look.

"She's in there. Has been for a week."

"So," Kronos interrupted them before it escalated like it always did, "if we can't approach it quietly, then we take a page from our brother's handbook. We walk right up to the front door."

He looked to Crius, who gave his agreement.

Oceanus did the same.

Then Rhea.

Hades was last and rolled his eyes.

"Yeah, great, I vote for the suicide mission too. That sounds fun."

We find ourselves looking at a doorway.

Artemis, Themis, Tethys, Mnemosyne, Hermes and me.

It's an unassuming entryway, a door set back in an alley about thirty feet. There's two burly men standing by the door, checking the patrons of the club in and out. When they aren't busy doing that they're talking to each other, chuckling and not really paying attention to their surroundings.

They should really be paying attention. This might not be as difficult as we thought.

"Are we just constantly wrong about how strong we are, even without the weapons? This all seems too easy," Tethys whispers into my ear and I honestly can't answer.

Maybe we assumed wrong. Maybe they weren't all that powerful. Maybe we were buying their lies about being gods instead of relying on the knowledge that *we are* gods.

"Don't think about that yet," I whisper back to her, "it's not the time to think about it. That's how mistakes happen."

I try to drive the thought of my own mind, but it occurs to me that Hermes has always been different. Faster than a mortal man should be. Gifted. Maybe some of these Olympians have something to them. Maybe that's how they stole our power.

How many gods can there possibly be? There must be a line drawn somewhere, there must be.

"We'll take them quiet," Hermes opens his mouth and speaks, I roll my eyes at him.

"The plan was to kick in the doors, no need to be subtle about those two."

I walk towards them, letting my chain unravel and drag on the pavement, the clattering links comforting to hear. It's also loud and obnoxious and gives me away well before I reach the two men. They freeze in place, as they should. They stand in the presence of a god.

The arrows that hit them come in quick succession and I feel the wind of them passing over my shoulders, one pinning a man to the brick wall and the other flung down the alley like a rag doll, as if struck by a hammer blow.

I turn, and Artemis just smiles as me.

"You were taking too long," she says, as if she's funny. I repeat the words but mock her with the highest pitch I can muster and walk to the door leading to the club and our dear Dionysus. She tries the handle, but it doesn't budge, they have some sort of heavy-duty lock set on the thing. She takes a strange device from her pocket and kneels at the door, fiddling with the lock.

I wait just long enough and then I strike with the chain. The door bends inward under the last link before the hinges give out and the whole mess crashes inward with the shrieking of metal on metal, crashing down a long flight of steps. I glance down the stairs and see that, luckily, no one was on the stairs. What are the odds?

I look to Artemis who doesn't look happy.

"You were taking too long." It feels good to throw the words back at her, oh does it feel good.

Themis leads the charge down towards the thumping music of the nightclub, Tethys and Hermes on her heels. I bow slightly and offer the doorway to Artemis while Mnemosyne waits for us to be done with the games. Artemis *tuts* at me as she runs off after the others.

"You missed her, didn't you?"

Mnemosyne says it to me and I don't answer her, there's too much to focus on for a distraction like that.

But yes. I did.

It didn't take long for the screaming to start once the door hit the bottom of the stairs and someone noticed us following suit. I suppose fame comes at the price of recognition. The man who created fire was coming and last time he and his friends showed up a few people ended up dead. That might scare the mortals, especially with their fears and insecurities about death.

Those who were there to live it up scattered first, fleeing from the main entry into the club itself where the music was still thumping away. Themis threw herself into the first thug to come around the corner and they fell together as she used a flurry of strikes to subdue him. Tethys launched her elemental at the next one, enveloping him in a clear bubble of water before tossing him into a wall with a loud *crunch* of breaking bones.

I hadn't seen Hermes fight in a very long. As we rounded into the club's first room I was witness to the graceful display that it was. There were at least half a dozen men moving to block us from going further. Some of them were already shooting as they moved but Hermes was too quick for that, he dodged to the left and slid along the floor to the first on the far left. He moved up, twisted the man's arm and then delivered a side kick to his knee. It shattered, and his leg collapsed inward as the man screamed in pain and clutched at a now useless leg. The second and third were moving to aim at Hermes but he was there, grabbing the second in line by the wrist and twisting his arm up and over his head and using a free hand to cause the thug to fire his pistol right into the third man's left eye.

He spun, using the second thug as a shield from the onslaught of gunfire, moving backward to the last three. They dropped empty magazines to reload but Hermes was right there. The fourth man had slammed his magazine in when Hermes grabbed the pistol and turned it, firing up into the man's chin and making a mess of the top of his head. He was moving for the last two when a single arrow pinned their arms together and they screamed until another pierced both their heads.

Artemis just couldn't let anyone have all the fun.

"That was easy," Hermes said, watching the two bodies drop to the floor together.

Oh, what fun.

We have only made it to the first of two main rooms that make up the club, I know from the blueprints that there are also at least two exits, a manager's office, and several storage rooms. Where we are now is just the first of many rooms to clear and still no sign of Dionysus, though people who came to party the night away have begun fleeing to the next room. That leaves us in an empty room lit by pulsing lights that would probably go very well with music. If there was any.

The next room is larger, much larger, and a VIP lounge overlooks the dance floor. Dionysus will be above us, and above is always the better place to be.

"Those double doors take us to him," Mnemosyne says as she enters after us. She was never much for the violence and bloodshed that we were more accustomed to. I think it has to do with remembering everything that she sees and does, seeing a life drain every moment can't be easy.

We don't get a chance to move before a series of enormous floodlights light up the room and heavy bars drop to close the entry and exits to us, bars that look an awful lot like Titanic metals. Gone are the pulsing lights and we are left in a brightly lit dance room. From a perch above us, Dionysus appears, holding a half empty glass of wine in one hand.

"Welcome to my world," he says into a microphone, slurring a little more than I remember. He could always hold his own in the drink, so that means he must be well into his stash by now.

"Dion," Mnemosyne speaks and no one else dares to, he was her friend and she will remember everything about him. It will be fresh for her. No matter how long it's been.

"Don't!" he shouts, sloshing wine out of the glass as he thrusts it at her. "Don't you 'Dion' at me. You, all of you, wanted everything! You took everything! Do you know how many people died? I do! Families butchered all for him!"

He points at me and I look down in shame. He's not wrong.

"You deserved to rot in that place! Zeus never should have concocted his scheme, that power-hungry fool is as bad as you were!"

"Dion, please," she begged him, "you don't have to do this. None of this. Come with us. Please."

He turned his back on her, drained his glass and yelled a short sentence that shot a pang of something I didn't remember through my chest. A strange feeling that took a moment to place. With the words Dionysus was gone and we were alone with the sound of metal shrieking as a hole in the floor opened before us. The music started in the next room as we were quickly forgotten to die here.

"Let Cerberus have them!" He had said.

As the hatch in the floor opened further I remembered what the feeling was.

It was fear.

I had always assumed that Cerberus hadn't survived all these years, we hadn't exactly made him with the intention of a long life, but we also hadn't really considered it either. I think that Kronos and I take a lot of the blame on his creation, with a little help from Coeus and some pilfered powers from Iapetus. Coeus had taken a scientific interest but Kronos and I had come up with the idea on one night after a great deal of wine. We had a few of those but this one sticks out.

A three-headed beast to guard the treasures of the Titans.

The problem with the plan was that we didn't have treasures. Other than our weapons there were no baubles or trinkets of the Titans. Those were mortal trappings not godly ones.

That hadn't stopped us at the time. Coeus had the know-how and Kronos had lifted a life orb that Iapetus had been working on. He massaged muddy earth into the shape of a dog and then I had laughingly suggested it be given three heads.

He did. Then we shoved the life orb inside and it was done. We had made life without consulting the master of life himself. It had been fine at first, Cerberus was nothing more than a playful puppy that followed me around. The problem was how quickly he grew, he started out just barely at my knee and by the time Iapetus found out his heads were as tall as my chest. Luckily, he stopped growing around then and Iapetus sort of just let us keep him.

Until everything changed, and we wound up in our prison.

This one is on me.

"When he comes out, let me deal with this, alright? If it goes sideways, step in but otherwise leave him to me," I say it and I get approval in return. I think Themis thinks it's the right thing to do and the others don't really want to get into a fight with Cerberus. I can't really blame them, I don't either.

He's the creation of the two most powerful elemental gods.

He can kill a Titan. He can kill me.

And if I'm honest with myself I'm not entirely sure I can kill him.

I don't have to wait long before I find out what my friend has become. Before the plate has fully opened two massive paws grip the tiled floor and the muscles and sinews of powerful limbs appear as he heaves himself up. His torso has more scars than I remember in the thick black fur, but I remember those bright red eyes, like looking at two smoldering embers embedded in a block shaped head. All three of them. He stretches himself out, at least three times as long as any man is tall, and I can remember him leaping the height of a full-grown tree on those powerful back legs.

Cerberus is the beast of Titans and I doubt he remembers me.

He has been in prison, or a slave, all while I was away. Neither is an appealing thought.

"I feel you pup," I whisper, gripping one end of my chain tighter.

He whips his heads around and locks all three pairs of eyes on me and each head snarls, lips curling back over rows of dangerous teeth and spittle dripping to the floor. He takes a few paces towards me, clearly having selected his target.

"Don't you remember me?"

He tilts his heads and the snarling stops. Maybe he does?

He launches off those back legs and hurtles through the air at me, clawed front paws held out and the snarling back. I move to the side but one of his claws tears through the meat of my upper arm up to my shoulder. It spins me to the floor, blood pouring from the wound. He continues through the leap and tumbles on the floor, regaining his footing to look at the damage.

I manage to get to my feet and look at my shoulder with the torn flesh and the pumping blood, it's not good.

He growls and sniffs the air, tongues flicking out to taste the blood on it.

"Come on, don't you remember me?" I yell it. He leaps again, this time I bring up the chain and slide underneath him, the chain tossing him over my head and onto his back with a chorus of yelps.

He regains his footing and looks at me angrily, growling low in his throat and eying the chain warily. He doesn't remember any of it. I hear the music from the next room and I swear I can hear Dionysus cheering and shouting above everything else.

Running away like a scared little rabbit.

A rabbit.

I drop the chain and it coils onto itself on the floor. Cerberus watches carefully, fearing a trap. He was always too smart for his own good. Full of energy too.

I kneel and ignore the shouts of the others, holding up a hand to stop them from intervening. Maybe it's the blood loss, maybe it's a stroke of genius, but this will work. Cerberus deserves a second life.

"Sit," I shout as firmly as I can manage, those damn claws did a number on me. He tilts his heads again and continues coming forward, slowly plodding on those paws. So, I do it. I concentrate all the power I have left into my hands and form the fire into a shape. It's got four legs and it nervously flits its head from side to side, long ears pressed back along its body. We used to play a game.

He stops moving towards me. Watching the fire merge and move through the shape of the animal. His favorite to chase through the forests, or it had been.

"Cerberus...sit!" I stand and shout it, this time it's loud and firm. His eyes bore into mine but slowly his back end drops to the floor. He hovers a bit and I raise my eyebrows at him and he watches me. He waits, waits, waits and then it hits with a *thump*. In his eyes I can see the confusion and I take the silence from my comrades to be their own surprise, but I don't have the nerve to look over, if I break eye contact it might all end.

I hold the rabbit and urge the fire to struggle, to try to escape from my grip though it cannot possibly do so. Three pairs of eyes watch it carefully with anticipation. That's when I see it. All the heads snap up and look at me. One by one they soften slightly and then their mouths drop open and tongues loll out. He makes a strange noise in his chest and shuffles on those massive paws. He eyes the rabbit and then me and I think, maybe even pray, that there's a flicker of recognition in those eyes.

"Come here," I say, hoping I'm not wrong. He charges forward. Mouths open, teeth flashing, I wince and wait for the tearing of flesh again.

The center of the three heads hits me in the chest and I go down. I embrace death as he…he licks me sloppily. A warm tongue slobbers over my face and he nuzzles me, whining and excitedly trying to force a nose between my hands to free the rabbit.

"Good boy," I say, closing my eyes and letting out an enormous breath of relief and open my hands. He chases the rabbit of fire and catches it easily, shaking it in one set of powerful jaws before all three clamp jaws around it and the shape explodes in a cascade of sparks into the air. He bounces and snaps at the floating fire just like I remember.

Blood drips to the floor in a veritable river of life force. Artemis is first to my side; the others close behind. She touches it and I pull back, glaring at her.

"Ow. That's an open wound, thank you."

She mocks me and pinches the tear shut, not gently. I grunt and whimper as a thick head pushes itself under my hand and Cerberus licks at the blood gently. Almost apologetically.

"I know boy, I know," I say, patting him, "wrap the chain around it." Themis and Artemis do as I ask, not kindly and I force a stream of power through the links around my arm. It hurts, and I scream as the fire courses through my torn flesh and stops the blood flowing from my body. When it's done I slump, feeling almost completely drained of power. I'm not meant to be underground, I need sunlight.

"Can you go on and handle this?" I ask of them and they seem to agree, that should be enough to handle whatever is through that door. At least I hope so.

"How do we get through that?" Hermes doesn't think big, obviously, or he'd have the answer to his own question.

"Like this."

I form another rabbit out of what little fire is left to me and Cerberus perks up, all three heads watching carefully at our old game. He sits, feet tapping in front of him in barely contained excitement.

"Are you ready?" I ask them, holding the rabbit tight between my hands as it tries to run.

They are. I let it run and Cerberus takes off after it. He's big and powerful, his muscles straining as he follows the rabbit and quickly gets up to speed. When the rabbit squirms and slips under the door that held us back Cerberus hits that door at that same speed. He was never one to hold back during the game, once knocking over a few trees in a forest when we had played many years ago.

Cerberus hitting the door was nothing short of thunderous and the whole wall shook. I saw the door give just a little and that was before Cerberus started pawing and digging at the bottom of the door, forcing it further and further in.

Then the door gave way.

And we were in.

Chapter XXV

Dionysus had made a name for himself in the Russian underground, both as a notorious partier and as a phenomenal money launderer. He owned dozens of clubs all over the world, but he always came back to the place where he felt safest. Or had felt safest.

If things didn't work out now he'd be done, for good.

"I always knew they would come back," he slurred, wrapping an arm around his current best friend and protégé, "I knew it. You can't keep power like that locked up, not for long. We got three thousand years, that's a good run. Right?"

His protege shrugged, he assumed Dionysus was just drunk rambling again, as was his way. After a few drinks Dionysus had forgotten that he hadn't shared any details with his protege. That's why when Dionysus pulled a short sword from under the table and laid it on top, his protege was visibly surprised.

Mnemosyne had used a disgusting sling, so primitive. At the first opportunity

Dionysus had the thing reworked into a sword, the sling wrapped around the grip and her pouch of metal shot forged into the blade.

He ran a finger over the length of the sword and drew a fine line of welling blood, reminding him of all that had come before. Dionysus looked at his protege and wondered if the boy had any idea that he sat near a good. Dionysus liked to keep business and pleasure separate and kept a great many secrets. Dionysus launched into a fit of giggles and raised his glass.

"My pleasure is business!"

His protege shook his head and went to get a few bottles of water, before the drinking had taken over Dionysus had been going on about people coming to kill him. The club was packed with people and thugs armed to the teeth on catwalks overhead and at all the doors. With someone like Dionysus it was only a matter of time before someone would want to kill him.

The DJ pumped up the crowd with a beat, the whole underground shaking with their feet stomping in unison, jumping up and down like fools. At least the drunk idiots paid well, he thought, looking back to Dionysus who was now busy telling his story to a man who didn't speak English but politely nodded along.

The outer edge of the dance floor sported massive iron bowls that currently weren't in use. He furrowed his brow and waved a hand to one of the bartenders until he got the other man's attention. He jabbed a finger at the bowls. The bartender held up his arms to say 'I dunno' so he jabbed his fingers again and made his best 'fix it' face.

He made it two more steps before there was a noise that drowned out the music for a moment and the club shook more violently than the jumping had done.

There was a brief spat of gunfire from the entrance and Dionysus stood from his VIP booth, shakily. Though he looked sober now.

He looked to his protégé and then slumped back down and drained his glass of wine.

"Time's up."

I stepped through after Cerberus took down the door, searching for the rabbit that he had chased after. Instead he found a busy dance floor that was now deathly silent and a handful of thugs with their weapons out.

When the first shot rang out the bullet sank into the meat of Cerberus' shoulder.

From there, things got worse.

Not for us.

Cerberus is too large, their weapons are designed for a man-sized target, not a Cerberus sized target. It sinks into his haunch but doesn't stop the three-headed beast. It just infuriates him.

Cerberus moves like a flash and closes one set of jaws on the man's chest and another on his legs. Then he does what dogs are prone to do and pulls the two halves apart. I can only hear the muffled screams and they don't last long.

Mortals are not built for that sort of punishment and his body gives out under the forces being put on it and it is truly disgusting. He tears in half around the waist and Cerberus tosses the halves in opposing directions with a wet noise.

There was a long pause in the room where the music stopped and every single patron stares in abject horror. There were strangers in their midst, blood soaked and horrific strangers with a three-headed dog that had just torn a man in half. That must be a sight.

At the end of the pause there is a noise that comforts me. There were various black urns scattered throughout the massive room and at that moment a bartender turned a knob. Dionysus rose from his booth and shouted something at the young bartender, but it was too late. He had turned it.

The urns came to life with flame, flickering as a pilot light ignited a thick fluid and sending bright blue flames into the air. It's not the sun but it is fire and that is good enough. Once it is in the air I can feel it on my skin, pinpricks rising on my skin as the energy crackles in each particle of air.

I think Dionysus had tried to shout "no" but it was too late. The searing pain in my arm instantly begins to fade, not as quickly as it would if it was the sun but quickly enough. The fibers knit themselves back together and I flex my fingers out as the numbness fades from them, feeling the muscles loosen and heal.

I stand beside Cerberus who growls at the remaining thugs and guards, who slowly back away from the three-headed dog that stands as tall as my shoulders.

Mnemosyne pushes past me and thrusts a finger at Dionysus on his balcony overlooking us.

She says something that I've never heard come from her mouth, something I never thought our sweet sister would say to any living being.

"I will kill you, you bastard!"

I'm proud of her.

"What are you waiting for!" Dionysus shouts back, throwing his glass at us weakly. "Kill them!"

The guards look at each other, then to Cerberus and to me and the rest of the Titans and Olympians that stand with us. They seem nervous.

They should be.

The first to go for his weapon, reaching for his armpit where a pistol hangs, is pierced by an arrow that pins his wrist to his chest. He would probably have screamed in pain if he wasn't dead.

"Good shot," I say to Artemis and she smiles at me, notching another arrow.

It doesn't take long before it's my favorite part of any day.

The part where the fighting starts.

There is chaos in the underground. I move quickly and strike down a man with a pistol, the chain bursting through his chest and back and snuffing out a life. Cerberus is beside me, growling and tearing through those bold enough to take on the oversized hound. Hermes and Artemis move like water in their own ways, Artemis light on her feet and loosing arrows as she does. Hermes is a flash of movement that hits like a hammer against an anvil. Tethys is between the two, her elemental flowing around her as she dances a path of death with the dagger, slashing and striking through.

It's in the lust for battle that we made our mistake.

Themis had allowed Artemis to keep her bow, the symbol of balance that she had been so skilled with. Tethys had her dagger and Hermes was clearly good with his hands and had some sort of training, he used discarded firearms in place of the dagger he had returned to Tethys. I have the chain and Cerberus needs no weapon.

Mnemosyne and Themis have no weapons, so they held themselves back from the line of fighting.

Or they should have. There was our mistake. Our critical error. Mnemosyne was furious with her friend and she took off towards his vantage point, weaving through the dancers. The guards didn't have to focus on her because they were busy enough with us. Only Themis saw her run off and only Themis gave chase.

Only Themis followed Mnemosyne up the stairs to the booth. Only Themis was there to fight with the two bodyguards alongside our sister, the two men that bravely and foolishly stood against two Titans. Even without weapons it was no contest.

I should have been there for them.

Dionysus was wobbling on his feet, Mnemosyne went at him first. An eternity of drinking had made him all but immune to the effects of it all. It was mostly for show. He wasn't stupid, even if he had made his living as the fool of the Olympians.

He was no fool.

Themis saw it before Mnemosyne did, probably being more aware and less clouded by anger.

I should have been there.

Themis pulled Mnemosyne away and to the side as Dionysus stopped wobbling, stopped the lie and thrust a blade from inside the lining of his suit jacket at Mnemosyne.

The blade flashed in the club's lights and time slowed to a crawl.

All the noise faded away, all the people faded away. There was only Mnemosyne's own Titanic weapon, forged into a blade, as it slid through Themis' chest. It slipped between her ribs and pierced her heart and Themis died on that balcony. She was snuffed out just like that.

There was no justice in it. No fairness.

I know all this because Mnemosyne cannot forget it. Every detail. Every moment.

Right up to when we found her alone on that balcony. She cradled Themis' head in her lap and wept.

I don't have her gift or abilities. I only have mine.

I don't remember how I got to the end. I don't know how I found him, but I did. I found him in an alley, trying to run for a car. I broke his leg with the chain. He fell to the ground screaming and I saw a blood covered blade skitter across the pavement.

I hear the faint screaming as I walk to him and turn him over with my foot. He clutches his shattered leg and looks at me with fear. He knows his mistake.

I hear him say something in a pleading tone. I tell him that begging doesn't suit him.

I turn him over onto his front and grab the back of his suit jacket, pulling him up to his knees. He shrieks as the destroyed bones in his bad leg grind and move. I ignore it. His car speeds away and his thugs desert him.

I lean down and whisper into his ear. I don't know what I'm going to say until I say it.

"You die alone."

I grip his chin and slam shut his mouth to end the screaming. I sink my knee into his upper back and press forward to apply firm pressure. I pull back with my hands and twist his head at the same time while pushing forward with my knee with all the force I can muster.

The snap echoes through the alley and the streets and the city itself.

I look up to see a small group watching from the end of the alley where the car had been, they have their devices out and are watching me with fearful but interested eyes. Vultures, craving a scene of death. They watch and record, only shrinking away when Cerberus finds me and sniffs at my hands and the blade. He whines softly and nuzzles my arm with one of those blockish heads and I scratch him.

"I know pup," I say, looking at the blood as my vision clouds with tears, "I know."

I leave Dionysus' body there in the alley, alone and to be forgotten. So dies a false god.

I only stop to retrieve the blade coated with Themis' blood.

I think I will remember this night as Mnemosyne will. It will always be clear. As I carry my sister out and we disappear into the night I only have one thought.

I should have been there.

Chapter XXVI

Demeter stood on the stairs leading to her expansive home, arms crossed as the group approached. Kronos and Rhea led the group, the first with jaw clenched and the other pacing beside her formidable lion. Crius, Oceanus and Hades walked close behind as they cautiously approached her.

They had simply walked to her door, boldly done.

Her property was dotted with ornate marble statues carrying swords and spears in various formidable poses of combat, striking pieces of art. The faded white contrasted against the manicured green lawn.

"You should have died in that hole," she shouted, turning on her heel and marching through the front doors. "I suppose here will have to do."

Kronos and the others had no time to react before sections of the perfect grass lifted around them and heavily armed troops leaped from the new holes and began shooting. At the same time the marble statues seemed to come to life, joints appearing as they moved arms and legs and descended their platforms.

Kronos raised his hands and called on the earth around them, raising up a fortification that surrounded them and absorbed the gunfire. He focused on the earth, strengthening it while the gunfire continued.

Rhea helped him, drawing veins of stone into the earthen wall from deep beneath their feet. She had just finished when a marble sword crashed through the wall and stopped only a few inches from her face, held in place by the earthen wall. The statues were Demeter's work, she was more powerful than they had expected.

Oceanus moved quickly and dropped the handle of the trident through the marble sword, shattering it.

A spear tip burst through the wall and grazed Hades' side. He grunted as blood started to seep out and glared at the others.

"Suicide mission!"

Hades said it angrily as he pulled the spear through the wall, gripping it by the handle and then pushing it back out the same hole. He was rewarded with the sound of marble grinding through marble.

There was a lull in the gunfire and they heard a muffled call for explosives.

"What's your plan?" Rhea looked to her twin brother, holding the veins of stone inside his earthen wall.

"Do you remember that day with the Giants?" He asked her, and she nodded, smiling slightly at the memory. They had been trapped by a few angry Giants after a mistaken foray into their territory. Before the truce. She remembered it well.

"Can we know the plan?" Hades moved to the side as the spear came back at him, this time the lion snapped it in half between powerful jaws. Hades looked at the stone lion.

"Show off."

Oceanus and Crius weren't against Hades' question, instead Kronos and Rhea closed their eyes and placed their hands flat against the wall of earth and stone. They blocked out everything else and waited for the vibration of one of the soldiers slapping an explosive charge against the barrier, it rippled through the defense.

Then the wall exploded outwards, shards of stone mixing with pieces of earth and becoming deadly shrapnel, the explosive device didn't get a chance to be detonated before the shard had either pierced the troops or tossed them to the ground with blunt force. The statues were largely unaffected, so Oceanus thrust the trident through the nearest while Rhea's lion threw its weight onto another and began to demolish it with weighty paws and powerful jaws. Hades brushed shattered marble pieces off his shoulder and checked his bleeding wound calmly.

"Well, I suppose we'll have to deal with them?"

Crius punched Hades in the shoulder and moved quickly towards the armed men that were struggling to get to their feet and retrieve their weapons.

"Shut up and do something."

Hades mocked him and kicked one of the soldiers in the chin, slamming his mouth shut with the top of his shoes with resounding crack and knocking the man unconscious. Crius delivered his own strike, a closed fist across the face, of another. While they handled the men, Oceanus and Rhea's lion continued struggling against the statues.

Kronos took the steps to the front door of the villa two at a time, entering a strangely quiet home. Rhea wasn't far behind him.

Kronos saw her standing there, Demeter, arms crossed and sitting in a pristine white chair with a recognizable sickle lying flat across her lap. She played with the blade, running a thin finger along the edge. She smiled coyly at the two of them.

"Well, Ares thought it was worth a try. I told him it was worthless, but he insisted. You know how stubborn that idiot is."

Kronos clenched his jaw and stared at her, gripping his lesser sickle so tightly his knuckles went white. Rhea stood back to let her brother work this out. It wasn't her place to intervene. The villa was empty but for the lithe woman sitting in the chair. Waiting patiently for this moment, so it would seem.

Demeter remained sitting as Kronos walked to her. She held up the sickle in the palm of her hand and he took it from her.

"Can't talk you out of it?" she said, watching him with a smirk.

He thrust the sickle into her stomach, letting the tip drive in and forcing the curved blade up into her chest. There it would pierce her heart and she would die, bleeding out in the perfect white chair.

She gasped, shocked and horrified, looking down and clutching at the blade slowly tearing through her flesh. There was no blood though and when she started laughing, Kronos knew something wasn't quite right.

She laughed harder and harder, standing from the chair. In a terrifying turn she began to melt, her flawless skin becoming a thick sludge of mud and earth along with the sickle buried inside her chest. Kronos stepped back as the woman he had loved once became earthen. The façade collapsed onto the floor and chair in an earthen mess.

"I'm disappointed, I thought you would have been smarter than that." Demeter's voice returned, this time from a crystal screen on a wall opposite the chair she had been sitting in. She idly picked at some dirt beneath her fingernails on the screen.

"I can't believe you thought I'd be sitting around waiting for you, not after that business with Poseidon. You got the attention of the world with that."

She leaned forward towards the camera and held up the real sickle then raised her middle finger to Kronos and Rhea.

"Now you get to find out the price of fame."

The screen went dark and she was gone. Kronos was about to say something to Rhea before Hades came in, pushing his hair back into place and looking unhappy.

"We've got a small problem," he said, looking back through the front door, "the town is on fire."

We sit in silence and no one wants to break it, not now. Hades' pilots are taking us to the safehouse where Phoebe and Coeus are safely hidden.

Themis' body sits in a seat, covered with a blanket for some shred of respect we can provide her. Mnemosyne hasn't spoken since she told us what had happened on that balcony, how they had ended up with Dionysus alone.

She sits blankly, staring ahead and playing the scene over and over and over again in her mind. I know she is because I would be. Any of us would be.

"It's not fair," Artemis says it to me quietly, just to me. She'd taken the seat next to me and I hadn't argued it. Tethys sat beside Themis' body, holding one hand and crying silently, staring out the window.

I don't have anything to say to those words.

All I could think about was how we had failed them both, how we should have been with them and we could have stopped it. How Themis did the right thing, but Mnemosyne would never forgive her for it, would never forget.

When Artemis said those three words it sank in for me, sank in that it wasn't fair. For Themis to be snuffed out like that wasn't right.

That wasn't justice.

First Theia, then Iapetus and now Themis. Titans were dying all because of me. The war that I had started three thousand years ago had led us to this point in time, every rash decision I had made and every ounce of power I had craved had brought us down.

It had killed my sister.

It had killed my brother.

It had killed our moral compass.

I had killed them all.

When the phone that Hades provided for me begins to vibrate in my pocket I am pulled from the thoughts that threaten to give way to a fiery rage. I remove the phone from my pocket and tap the green button with my finger for the unknown number, holding it to my ear to hear Ares' voice. A voice I hadn't heard for a long time. He and I had always got along well, though he struck me as a bit on the slower side. What Iapetus had seen in that one was always a mystery.

"Dionysus? That's an interesting choice for you. Did you know that you're all over the news?"

I hold back the anger and engage, wondering who I am. I would normally have threatened to pull his innards out through one orifice or another but…I suppose that's growth.

"Ares, come to beg for your life? Grovel? Make a deal?"

Ares simply laughed at that. It was worth a try, even if it was a long shot. He's too stubborn, maybe even too stupid to make the right decision.

"Not quite, I have someone who wants to talk to you."

I heard weak breathing take the place of his voice, a rattling breath that sounded like it belonged to a very hurt person. Then she spoke.

"Hyperion," it sounded like Hestia but at the same time it didn't, like she was talking through a mouth of broken teeth and swollen tissue. I don't know what to say to her. My sister's confidant and friend does not sound good and I have a feeling I know where this is going. I don't think it's going anywhere good.

"Hestia…she's gone."

I hear her breath catch and she chokes out a sob before the phone is taken away from her.

"Ares, you can still stop this."

I hear the phone being set down, a choking sob and a gunshot.

Then Ares returns.

"See you soon."

There is nothing but silence as the call is ended.

I look up to see that everyone has been watching me, that they could only hear the one side of the conversation. They could hear the gunshot though.

I throw the phone down the length of the plane where it shatters on the cockpit door.

One of the pilots opens it and glances back then quickly shuts the door again when he sees the broken phone. I stand and storm the length of the aisle and then stop, screaming at the back of the plane. It's a bestial sound that I haven't heard in a long time.

I scream until I don't feel helpless, until I don't feel weak, until everyone has backed away from me in fear and the light burns outside the small windows as the sun feels my rage. That's all I have for now.

So, I scream.

She was a young woman, wearing the habit of a nun and walking the streets. Children gathered at her hem and she whisked up one into her arms, the whole group giggling along with her as she did. A well-known figure in the community, Hestia had all but pushed thoughts of the Olympians and Titans from her mind. She had taken up the mantle of helping where she could and doing what good she could in the world, spiriting away Theia's weapon to a corner of the world that none of the Olympians would dare tread in.

She turned a corner and shooed the children off, having work to attend to at the small convent where she was to serve dinner for the community later in the evening. There was no place for the little ones around the bustle of the kitchen, they had enough volunteers who came to repay the kindness of the nun they had come to love.

All Hestia had to do was cross through a single alley. An alley that was almost too quiet for the midday bustle of the city.

The hair on the back of her neck stood straight and she tensed, she had never been one for combat though she'd learned a few tricks along the way. She didn't know if the Olympians would leave her alone but why would they come now?

"Who's there?" she called out softly, hoping to draw the unseen figure out from the shadows of the alley.

It worked.

She immediately relaxed and ran to the woman, embracing her tightly and choking out tears of joy. They hadn't seen each other in a very long time.

"How did you find me?" Hestia asked, gripping the other woman's hands tightly. The woman smiled at her.

"I never lost track of you in the first place."

Hestia smiled and checked the alley for any untoward eyes that might watch them, hurrying the other through the alley towards the safety of the convent.

"Come, quickly, we'll talk somewhere safe."

As they walked together, the woman said something to Hestia.

"I need your help, badly."

"Of course," Hestia answered without hesitation, "anything."

"I need to know where the children are. I need to find the Titanic children."

Chapter XXVII

Phoebe sat in a darkened room, sitting in the pressing silence as she played out the future. She had shut the door, only responding to Jeff's questions about her well-being with calm gratitude and sealed herself away.

She could see the paths forming as decisions were made, actions were done that could never be undone, she felt the pain of the people that were suffering. That one was always going to happen, it was just a matter of how.

She sat, propped up by pillows on the bed with her eyes closed until the door opened slowly and quietly. Apollo entered the room and sat down on a chair to stare at her.

"I thought the door was obvious enough, so let me spell it out. Get out."

He didn't move. She opened her eyes and stared at him, eyes boring into his. He didn't look away and it made her furious.

"Not of all us were part of it." Apollo says, still looking at her.

"I am aware of that." Phoebe didn't say it with malice or fury or anything except a cold detachment. That was her way.

"The one who knows everything." She saw Apollo's eyes flash with something and she watched it all play out. Every path. The one where he throttled her on the bed, the one where he left without saying anything more, the ones that made her blush. Apollo was one of the few that could understand what it was like.

"Not all of us were a part of it, though we all played some part." His voice was softer this time and Phoebe could hear the pain there. She couldn't know which reality theirs had been, not while she'd been locked in Tartarus, but none of them were enviable.

She took a deep breath and reminded herself of that.

"Hades was the only one that stood up to them." He offered it without prodding and the picture started to clear in Phoebe's head. There were so many futures that could have been. Knowing the past limited them.

"They took Hestia, threw her down in front of him and threatened to cut her open right there." Apollo's eyes were distant as he spoke. "She told him not to give in. To take the weapons and hide them, to run. He couldn't. They were unkind to him. To say the least."

Phoebe felt the picture grow clearer. She saw Hades taking a brutal beating from Zeus and Ares, their fists falling as he laughed in their faces. As he taunted them.

She also saw Apollo and Athena stand by and let it happen.

"Hades was the only one to stand up to them. He tried for years to open Tartarus. Centuries. He thought it was his duty." Apollo wiped at his eyes and stood. "It was all of ours and we failed. Hades and Hestia hid the children."

It snapped more clearly into focus as he spoke. Phoebe understood what he was doing. He had seen it already. She was seeing so many futures that she couldn't reliably know what had happened, but he hadn't been locked away. He knew.

And she saw it happening. She saw Hades leading the children away from harm, burying his helmet in a safe place, building his underground empire for one purpose. She saw him holding Hestia's fingers between his, gently. She saw him laughing, smiling.

She saw Hestia die.

She didn't realize Apollo had left for some time. She didn't realize she'd been clutching the sheets so tightly they were tearing.

She saw all the death that was to come, and she saw all the death that had happened before. Cities burned for Zeus' greed. An entire civilization was annihilated from history, everything the Titans had worked to build was destroyed.

They had been imprisoned and that had ushered in a dark and forgotten age.

She could not know what was to come, not for certain.

She only knew that she didn't want any of the futures to come to pass.

There was only death.

Kronos, Oceanus, Rhea, Crius and Hades raced to the burning village that lay below Demeter's villa, leaving behind an utterly ruined villa. They could hear the distant screaming as flames swept through the buildings and drove innocents into the streets. Some rushed into the flames for family members or children, others tried to find safety.

"Oceanus!" Kronos shouted but his brother was already off towards the coastline, carrying that silly golden trident.

"We'll get people out!" Hades led Crius away towards the nearest group of people who were busy trying to get back into a burning building. There was screams of terror coming from behind the growing wall of fire.

"That bitch," Kronos hissed the word through clenched teeth and watched the flames spread from house to house, business to business, people running from the spreading fire. He was overwhelmed as the devastation unfolded. Rhea touched his shoulder.

"Start in one place and just move," she said, and he took a moment to gather himself. She was right. Pick a direction and go. He picked a direction and went for the nearest house where an older woman screamed for help. He couldn't understand the words she was saying but she was pointing into the flames hysterically.

It didn't take long to hear the muffled sounds of someone beyond the flame, someone calling for help. A child.

Kronos didn't think, he just stepped right into the flames without hesitation. He called up the earth around his feet and the woman screamed louder, backing away right into the snout of Rhea's lion which only caused her to scream louder If she kept it up she would faint. Kronos ignored it as he pushed through the flames, wishing with all his being that Hyperion was there. Fire never bothered him. This would have been easy with Hyperion.

Burning rubble pelted his face and he pushed through it, kicking aside debris and coughing as smoke choked his lungs. An eternity passed before he found the small body of a child, clutched in the arms of her father. Her father was unconscious, bleeding from a head wound where debris had struck him. Kronos pushed aside smoldering materials and scooped the two of them up, making his way back through the choking smoke and fire.

He looked up as the building groaned, pieces collapsing quicker than he would have liked.

Then the roof fell in.

Rhea tore into the rubble, her lion tossing aside beams as she dug through and the citizens of the town gathered around them. Oceanus had arrived from the sea, bringing with him an almost sentient flow of water that snaked into the flames and doused them, smoke and steam billowing into the sky as the fires went out. Crius and Hades were busy helping dig through other piles of rubble while emergency services and citizens dove in beside them, casting sideways glances at the pair. These strange men seemed to find enormous chunks of concrete and twisted metal or burned wooden beams light and easy to move, their strength greater than any man they had ever seen.

It was the lion that made everyone stare the most, a living beast of rock and fire. That was a new one for everyone in the town. Likely for any mortal anywhere. Rhea was trying to get into the now collapsed building that Kronos had gone into. As the flames were quenched by the seawater, she redoubled the digging efforts until a beam gave way to an earthen mound that looked out of place in the rubble. She placed a hand on it and it cracked under her touch, then crumbled away to reveal Kronos with a little girl and her father.

There were cheers from the crowd, many hands carrying their unconscious forms away from the collapsed building and to safety.

Kronos dragged himself out, covered in soot and coughing from the smoke but still more concerned about the two he'd gone in for.

Everyone had given up their fixation with the lion and instead looked to the massive man with the golden trident, the one that commanded the water and sported a tangled black beard.

"Poseidon!" someone said loudly but reverently as they approached him cautiously. He threw his head back and laughed, loud and long and from deep in his belly. He shook his head and locked eyes with the person who had said it.

"Oceanus," he corrected them.

If Hyperion had brought the world's attention to the man in the flames, that sentence was fuel for that fire. A lot of fuel.

Zeus was watching the videos sweep across the globe, videos that had started at almost nothing. It was no longer nothing. It was a movement.

There was a video of Oceanus correcting the people and that was all it had taken for things to get out of hand. There was no more secrecy, the hidden gods were no longer hidden. It didn't help that the men who had set the fires had been captured very quickly and almost immediately sold out Demeter's assistant as the one who had paid for them to set the fire. She was well known in the area.

She was much disliked in the same area.

"That was your plan!" Zeus shouted it, lunging from his chair and hitting her across the face with a meaty fist, knocking Demeter out of her chair and they both fell to the floor. Demeter drove the tip of her sickle into Zeus' throat while he wrapped his hands around her throat and started to squeeze. The others pulled them apart before one of them ended up dead.

She had nothing to say, her plan had backfired spectacularly. It was going to make the Titans into global pariahs, instead they were becoming gods again. The televisions continued with the spreading news coverage and in the crowds behind the droning idiots she could even see some mortals wearing t-shirts or waving signs of support.

"This is just the beginning, it's only going to get worse from here."

"No godsdamned shit." Ares offered up to the group, staring at the screens playing out their nightmare. The world was watching the Titans come out of their hole and the world was much more accepting of that sort of thing. Mortals weren't afraid of the things that went bump in the night, not anymore. Now they sought it out, they bought cameras and brought friends to hunt down the things beyond belief.

"This is bad." Zeus mumbled to himself, trying to think of a way to head it off, "this is very bad."

"What if we did the same thing?" Hera said, "what if we head off their popularity by coming out on our own?"

Zeus stared at her and blinked.

"We'll come out to the mortals? And say what? Hey, I'm Zeus, I've built an energy company by undercutting my enemies and closing their companies? Oh, and Poseidon is dead, but before he was he sank a few ships full of innocent men to build his! Hera? She's been abducting people to do research on how we can live longer! She's so good at it that the CIA used to call her up for torture advice. Ares? Ares has killed more men than the fucking black death over his life. Yes, kneel before us and praise us for we are the worst shits on the face of this planet."

Hera looked down as Zeus raised his voice, slamming his hands on the desk and building to a dull roar.

"Maybe we'll tell them about Hestia, a fucking nun that we cut up just to get information? Hermes? Who's spent his life on the run from us but still manages to take time to help people the world over. Artemis, I mean she's a serial killer but who's going to be mad when they found out she's tracked down murderers and rapists for her whole life to deliver justice? Tell me Hera, WHEN SHOULD WE COME OUT TO THE PEOPLE?"

He heaved, breathing in and out so heavily that it seemed as if the air pressure was changing in the room. The air particles crackled with energy and the collective remembered why Zeus was in charge. He possessed power from each Titan and when he lost his cool completely he had a temper to rival Hyperion himself.

No one had anything to say in response to the outburst as Zeus sat again. He gathered himself, smoothed his suit jacket and took a deep breath. He rubbed at the split skin on his knuckles from the hit on Demeter, who was rubbing a spreading bruise from the strike.

She glowered at Zeus while everyone else sat there in an awkward, heavy silence. Ares wasn't sure if this was how they had wanted things to go, Iapetus had sold him on a plan, but that plan had not involved two Olympians being killed.

"I'm sorry," Zeus said, taking deep breaths to calm himself, "just a little on edge."

Demeter tilted her head, though Ares was certain she wasn't doing so from forgiveness and just more so as a show. He leaned forward.

"So, it was a mistake," Ares said, drawing all eyes to him, "too late to change it now. We can't come out to the public. He's right on that. We also can't let them take the spotlight."

"What do you suggest then," Demeter snapped at him, "we tried it your way, we threw soldiers at them and used up power to take them on. They are Titans, they are stronger than us, faster, better. And they have help. So, enlighten us."

"We know where they're hiding," Ares said, leaning forward and smiling. Not a kind smile. The smile of a warrior. A cool and violent smile.

Chapter XXVIII

Coeus had not shown any sign of recovery to Athena, who did not have Mnemosyne's ability to prod into memories nor Coeus' level of knowledge. She had spent much of the time away from Tartarus wondering what her mentor would have become after all the years. She had not given much thought to the pain it would cause him to be sealed away for nearly three thousand years.

Now he was a husk, almost void of anything that had been what made Coeus. He stared ahead and didn't acknowledge her.

She had spent days trying to find his mind again but hadn't even received a single word in reply. She had brought him the deep literature of the new world they lived in, pages upon pages of information from the internet, anything that would have been the perfect fit for him when he had been at his peak.

It hadn't worked.

Apollo gathered her for a break to step away from Coeus for a moment, she needed a moment to think. She needed to not be staring at her failures in the flesh. She needed a break.

Coeus was left alone in the comfortable room as night drew ever closer, as the night will. His blank stare was broken for a moment when he heard gentle words being spoken somewhere down the hall. He slowly pushed himself from a sitting position on the edge of the bed and shambled down the hall, eyes unfocused but still he was drawn to the sounds.

The door was only slightly open at the end of the hall and a lamp burned bright from within, where Jeff lay on a bed with one of his daughters under his left arm, his wife and second daughter under his right. He awkwardly held a children's book and read from it to both small figures as they slept.

Coeus tilted his head and listened to the story, pushing open the door and sitting on the floor beside the bed to listen. Jeff didn't pause but squeezed his wife to tell her it was okay, glancing sideways at the Titan enraptured by the story.

Athena returned to find the room empty and panicked, racing to check other rooms until she found him again. Sitting cross-legged on the floor and listening. He was still staring ahead but she felt that maybe there was a change in him.

Maybe there was hope.

Hermes tells us that Hades and the others are already at Aphrodite's safehouse, protected and having failed in their search for Demeter. There's quite the news story around it, according to him, but he suggests we wait to find out from them directly.

Good enough.

Cerberus did not take kindly to the plane and finding a space for him in the available vehicles was no easy task either.

I don't look forward to the reunion, not at all. I must inform them that Themis was killed because I wasn't there, because none of us were there. I will bear the guilt of that inaction to a group of my siblings and tell them that one more of us has died. Mnemosyne will bear the memory. Others will bear the pain.

But I will carry the guilt.

I carry her body to the door and there is a heavy silence that hangs in the air while no one speaks, just a few startled gasps and some choked sobs. Our sister was a strict, morally upright sort and it was an injustice for us to outlive her.

At least that's how I felt. We were losing the better Titans and those of us remaining were being filled with violence. I carry her inside and lay her body on a couch so that we can each pay our respects, say some sort of goodbye.

One by one, in our own ways, we say goodbye to her. I am the last one, because I am the one that does not want to say goodbye. It means acknowledging the failure, my failure. Everyone seems to sense it and files out of the room, leaving just me and her there.

I kneel beside her and run my hand through that short hair, over her placid face. She could be sleeping. If not for the lack of breathing or movement of any kind.

She is gone.

"I am sorry," I whisper into her ear. "It is not justice."

She doesn't respond, though I almost expected her to. Her silence used to be a comfort as she pondered the right and wrong of whatever the situation was. Now her silence speaks to her absence.

I am surprised by movement in the room when Coeus walks in. I look at him expecting that blank look in his eyes. It's changed, not much but it's changed. He isn't muttering to himself like I'd seen before but he's not all there either. He kneels beside me and looks to Themis, his face immensely sad.

"Can't forget," he says to me, placing a hand gently on mine. Then he lowers his voice and for a fleeting moment I see Coeus behind those empty eyes, just a flash of him.

"Justice," he says to me. Then Coeus is gone again.

He leaves the room. He doesn't leave it empty though. He leaves me with a task. His statement was an order, an instruction.

"Come on." Cerberus perks up and tails me as we leave the house and disappear into the night, without a word to the others. It is time that I started acting like a Titan, like a god. There is no need to explain myself to them nor do I feel that I must.

There is a pretender out there that deserves death and I will visit it upon him, as is my right. I must leave the others behind to take care of this. They would understand but they would try to stop me. I can't allow that.

I have just one word in my mind.

Justice.

Chapter XXIX

I can only imagine the chaos once they realize that I have gone. I must admit that I am sad to miss it. Kronos will be furious as he begins the search for his missing brother.

Cerberus plods lightly beside me and I am comforted by this familiarity.

"Just like the old days," I say, scratching one of his chins as he licks my forearm with one rough tongue. In this darkening night I feel purpose again, I feel like a Titan.

"You think you were just going to disappear?"

I stop in my tracks and turn slowly to see her. She carries a bow on her back and stands with arms crossed. She looks perturbed.

"Some watchdog," I grumble to Cerberus and he simply pants at me in reply. Always the conversationalist.

"Where do you think you're going off to?" Artemis asks of me and I already know I will not be able to go anywhere without her. Short of killing her, there's no way I know of to keep her off my trail. Cerberus does not help in that regard, he's easy to follow.

"I'm going to kill Zeus. Like I should have gone to do in the first place."

She walks close to me, looks me in the eye and squints as if judging the validity of my decision. Themis had chosen well who she would play mentor to. Then Artemis shrugs, smiles and starts walking in a far different direction than Cerberus and I had been travelling.

"You'll need a guide, you're already going the wrong way."

Cerberus nuzzles my arm and snorts.

"I know," I said to him, "you were right."

He chuffs, happily, and bounds off to walk beside Artemis who scratches under one of his chins vigorously and says something rude to him about me.

And I can't help but smile.

"He's gone?" Kronos wanted to shout but he had been told that Jeff was threatening to kill the next Titan that woke his children. Bold statement from the man but he had earned it. The night had already become impossibly complicated with so many gods under one roof.

Hades had dubbed it "the worst family reunion I never wanted" and had gone to sit outside and smoke his way through a pack of cigarettes. The barely controlled chaos the unfolded inside Aphrodite's safehouse was growing by the minute and the ground itself seemed to shake in time with Kronos' frustration.

"Enough!" Rhea hissed it, not wanting to raise her voice. It earned an instant silence from everyone in attendance.

"He. Is. Gone." She emphasized it for the benefit of those who may be hard of hearing, "It's done. What do we do about it?"

"Well..." Oceanus started to answer but she glared at him. He slammed his mouth shut just after saying the word, realizing that had been a rhetorical question and not one that needed an answer. He wisely took a seat and kept his mouth shut for the rest of the one-sided conversation.

"We are lucky he stayed with us as long as he did," Rhea said, once she felt safe there would be no more interruptions from any of the others. "We'll find him again, it won't be hard. I'm sure he's going off somewhere to set something on fire."

"He's two blocks away, Artemis is with him."

The whole room turned to stare at Hades who was dragging a finger over his phone. When he finally looked up it was to a room of staring Titans.

"What? You really need to start using your phones, there's all sorts of handy stuff on there. Calculator, imperial to metric conversion, e-reader, Google, GPS tracker, tons of stuff. Music and movies too. It's really time to step into this century – ow!"

Rhea punched him in the side and took his phone, looking at the digital map of the area with the two blue dots that indicated Hyperion and Artemis. It took less than half an hour to get to the markers and find out that the phones were sitting on a curb, left behind.

Hyperion and Artemis were gone.

Hera and Demeter had an idea, not necessarily one that Zeus or Ares would have agreed with, but they had an idea nonetheless. Ares was busy planning some violent excursion with a handful of men he had hand-picked, sadistic types with a penchant for violence. Exactly the type of men both Hera and Demeter despised. They were blunt instruments that laid bare enormous wounds and carried inherent risk of being too loud, too noticeable, and too prone to failure.

Hera had cautioned a thousand times before that the men they were using simply believed themselves to be superior because of their training or the skills they did possess. They were formidable warriors in the world of mortals.

Against Titans? They were pawns to be sacrificed and nothing more. Not the lynch pins that Ares believed them to be.

That's why Hera had always been a much bigger fan of Ares' master. Mentor was not the word she would use for Iapetus, not even close. He lived for power, he craved it. He had tricked his family into believing the lie that it was life that he served, when it was death that he wanted most.

He and Hera had bonded over that. Both had lied to get where they wanted to be.

Demeter was more self-serving, but she functioned well in their plans. The three of them, Iapetus still using The Colonel's body, walked the pristine hallways of a biomedical research facility headed by one world renowned doctor. It was Hera's own creation, a vast enterprise of picking and prodding at mortal flesh to determine which secrets lay beneath.

Iapetus had backed her project. He received a steady supply of death to slake his thirst for mortal souls while Hera searched for a cure to the ailment that plagued the Olympians.

The Olympians were dying.

It was faster now that the Titans were shoving blades into hearts or snapping necks, but it had been happening before all that. Zeus had gone against all wisdom and pursued the solution to the problem by opening Tartarus. Hera would have preferred cracking open Aphrodite's ribcage and seeking the answers in a mess of Titanic internal organs, but Zeus was afraid of her for some reason. She would have even settled for their children. Iapetus was willing to give up his sons but for the fact that he didn't know where they were.

The uprising had not been without bloodshed. Not all Guardians of Tartarus had been willing to rebel against their gods and many had died for them. In the end it hadn't stopped anything from happening the way they had planned. It had just slowed progress.

That was Hera's mantra and deepest belief. That was why she had gone against the Titans. She was certain this was progress.

That the old gods must be eradicated to make way for the new, just as almost every pantheon believes.

Two pairs of heels clicked in the empty hallway, Iapetus' shoes made a less intrusive noise on softer rubber soles.

The facility was almost entirely empty of the regular employees, having been instructed to not be there during this process. It was too sensitive for them to even accidentally stumble on it.

The three of them entered an elevator and rode it down to the depths of the research facility, exiting on a floor marked "Cold Storage" and "Authorized Personnel Only" on two pristine signs. Hera took pride in her facility, she had wanted more time to prepare at Tartarus when they began building a facility to dissect Titans. If she'd had more time maybe none of this would have happened.

Zeus just had to push his luck and it was always running out.

She swiped her pass card and a set of doors *whooshed* open. She allowed Iapetus and Demeter to go in first since both had been to this floor before.

"How has it been coming along?" Iapetus said, more used to The Colonel's body now that it had been several weeks.

"Very well. The subject shows remarkable regenerative abilities. We've been testing him thoroughly for weeks, since we found him, and it looks like we've managed to make an enormous stride." Hera never imagined she'd become so clinical when talking about a living being.

Times had changed.

She had changed with them.

"We used genetic material taken from him and applied it into various mortal test subjects. Various ages, races and with different medical conditions."

"Willing subjects?" Iapetus asked, though he could guess the answer.

"Some." Hera led them to a viewing room, not unlike the ones in Tartarus. Below was a young man with a formidable physique. He hung loosely from a table raised to a moderate angle, his body strapped down by the restraints from Tartarus itself. He was asleep or unconscious, whichever it was made no difference to Hera.

"He's impressive," Demeter breathed out. Hera pushed a button on a panel at the bottom of the window.

"Just wait."

Moments later the door to the cell opened and three people entered, two men and a woman. One of the men wore a lab coat while the other two were dressed in composite body armor. They had studded their armor with polished metal, Iapetus found himself staring at the armor and wondering why it looked so familiar.

"Hoplites," Hera offered, catching his stare. "They did it themselves."

He didn't have time to ask before the man in the lab coat snapped a package under the nose of the figure strapped to the table. The figure lifted his head slowly and smiled, showing a row of perfect teeth as nonchalantly as he could muster.

"Mornin' doc," he said, twitching his nose, "you can always just ask me if I'm awake."

The doctor stepped out of the room and the door closed behind him. The two Hoplites remained. Demeter and Iapetus stood in the viewing room looking down at the boy. Hera hit another button and they could see the man on the table look up, suddenly able to see through the once opaque glass.

"Hera!" he said, grinning again. "So good to see you. Been a few days, having trouble? Rumor is there's a tiny little Titan problem bugging you all. I see you brought friends! Must be my lucky day."

Hera snapped her fingers at the two Hoplites and they turned their attention to the young man, beginning to circle the raised table.

"Do we have to do this?" Iapetus could see the moment of weakness flash across the young man's face, the boy had almost pleaded before the bravado came back. When the restraints opened, the young man hit the floor with a heavy thud. His legs weren't working too well yet, he fell forward but caught himself before his face hit the floor. He was tensed and ready for whatever came next.

The Hoplites closed in on him and the room became a frenetic combat zone. It was a flurry of punches and kicks, martial prowess on full display as the Hoplites laid into the man with their fists and feet. The young man moved well, blocking and dodging but he couldn't deliver a hit on the Hoplites. That wasn't for lack of trying.

He came close a few times, until one of his punches lingered a little too long. The male Hoplite ducked under it, gripping the young man's wrist and driving his shoulder up. Iapetus heard bones break.

The female Hoplite took the opportunity and drove a small knife from her boot into the prisoner's back. Together the Hoplites lifted him back to the table and strapped him down. Blood poured from the wound, down to his foot and dripped to the floor. His arm was bruising and sat awkwardly.

"Was that necessary?" Demeter said, picking at her nail, "you could have just told us whatever it is you found."

"Just watch." Hera said. They obliged.

It took less than thirty seconds for the blood to completely stop flowing as the wound stitched itself together. If not for the blood that stained his side and leg, there wasn't the faintest sign of the wound. He didn't even grunt in pain as his shoulder knitted itself back together shortly after.

"He heals as a Titan might but without a power source. That is his gift from his father."

Hera looked to Iapetus, who looked back at her without much concern.

"Did you find the other?"

Hera's lip curled just for a moment, disgusted by the thought of the brothers she had captured. It had taken an immense amount of work.

"They killed six Hoplites, I don't have an unlimited number of them."

"You do now," Iapetus said, motioning to the young man. "With his blood you can make an army."

The glass was opaque again. The young man was busy eyeing the two Hoplites that had just wounded him. He grinned again, those perfect teeth shining.

"We'll get out of this. One of us, both of us. When we do…we're going to rip you apart. Piece by bloody piece. Just you wait."

He leaned his head back, closed his eyes and let out a long breath of air.

Iapetus watched his son and felt nothing. How could one feel something for a child that turned on them?

Prometheus had been snatched as a baby, so he might never find him. There were two that he did know, that he had raised. They had been captured by Hera.

Menoetius was prideful, even strapped to the table and regularly tortured for his blood. A half-Titan has power. The other they had captured was a testament to just how powerful they could be.

He turned back to Hera.

"Take me to Atlas."

Hera's smile was slow as it crossed her face, clinical.

"Would you like to see your body first?"

Chapter XXX

She was a fit figure, with long brown hair that had been braided and pulled back. Even in the dark, her cloudy gray eyes sparkled. A long bow was strung over her back and a quiver of arrows was belted firmly to her thigh with fletching poking from perfectly balanced shafts of wood. She was old school, no composite. She didn't need anything like that.

She sat on her haunches as the darkness deepened and the night drew in. Her muscles screamed their discontent. She ignored them, breathing slowly and evenly while watching shadows flit about in the darkness, none of their forms distinguishable. Streetlights should have cast a low glow over the street on any given night, but they were simply dark on this one. That was not by accident.

This week left the street silent but for a handful of latecomers walking from the library or evening classes while the remainder were tucked safely in their rooms to cram the last bits of knowledge before their finals began. For the past two years, this length of roadway had gained a rather unflattering reputation among those students.

"Don't walk alone at night during finals week," was the advice the school had given. They offered their guardian of the night in the form of an overweight and underpaid guard that could only do so much, he tried his best and Artemis admired that in the guard. He just couldn't do it by himself. At some point he would have to take a bathroom break or escort a group of students that would leave yet another helpless and alone.

That was when he acted, at least historically. This unknown man moved in the night and offered his help. He would keep them safe and he was disarming and unassuming but not charming, the right blend of neutral and kind.

She had overlooked him the past year and she'd been too late the first. He was in his last year now and that meant she might lose the chance to stop this. She perked up at the sound of a low voice and a light laugh, both distinct. He had made his move.

She checked the watch on her wrist, there was a fifteen-minute window where the guard took his break and got a late-night coffee like clockwork. This was that window.

Her muscles almost sighed in relief as she stood, leaping from the roof to another to follow the muted voices. They were walking slowly and cautiously while carrying on a disarming conversation about world history, the kind of dry and boring conversation that puts people at ease.

He was gifted at this, his own form of hunting. She was disgusted by what he did with this gift, perhaps he would have made an excellent law enforcement official or investigator, a phenomenon of criminology. Instead he had become a monster.

Artemis was also a gifted hunter, she'd had years of experience in it and she had turned her hunt to him.

She was less than a shadow in her movements, lithe and graceful as she moved from roof to roof and followed the two shapes in the darkness. She could feel it in the voices, in the air itself. He was going to make his move. The young woman was no longer safe.

Artemis' feet hit the grass lawn of one of the houses as she dropped from the roof, her feet making little sound as she took long leaping strides to cover the distance just as the man drew a knife from the back of his pants. He would press the back of the blade to this young woman's throat and tell her to keep silent. Then he would take her into the darkness and in a few days her body would be found.

He delivered a heavy punch to the side of her head to disorient the young girl. Artemis would not let this one be taken.

Not this time.

Before he could bring up the blade Artemis was there, gripping his wrist with an iron grasp and twisting his wrist up. She slammed her free forearm against his wrist and it shattered under the violent blow. Artemis moved quickly and before the knife had dropped to the ground she delivered a blow with the knife edge of her hand to his throat to silence him before he could sob out a pained scream. He fell to his knees, trying to soothe both his shattered wrist and crushed throat.

While he struggled for air, Artemis planted a hand over the girl's mouth before she could scream.

"He won't hurt you," she said calmly, watching the panic leave the girl's eyes, "not now."

Artemis heard a familiar engine approaching and the headlights filtered through the darkness. This young girl was safe.

When the headlights came close the guard found a young girl kneeling in the street by a discarded knife, crying. He knelt beside her and told her the things he was supposed to, that she was safe now and it would be okay. To tell him what had happened.

It didn't take long for the flashing blue and red lights of the police to arrive where they took the girl's statement. Where the young man had gone was a mystery.

Until a few days later, in the same area that had found the other bodies they found a new one.

A young man, whose body was pinned to a tree in the vast forest with an arrow.

Artemis had acquired a vehicle for us, one with enough space for Cerberus. It had folding seats.

How very practical.

We stuffed ourselves in, abandoned our phones to avoid being followed, and began a drive towards Zeus. It hadn't taken long before she'd told me about life outside of Tartarus, from her perspective. She had taken the lessons from Themis to heart and focused on justice.

"Unique way to deliver it," I had quipped. She snorted at me, drily.

"Only way."

Can't argue with that logic.

There is a very long silence that lingers between us, at least an hour passes. I've almost fallen asleep with my head leaning on the window when I hear her voice.

"You haven't asked about them."

I slowly lift my head and stare out into the night, listening to the tires rumble on the highway and glancing at the passing lights of the few other travelers that share the road with us. I knew it would come up eventually. How could it not?

"Where are they?" I ask, it's the only question that I have.

"France. Apollo and Athena took them there. They're safe."

I spent nearly three thousand years in a prison of my own making. The day I felt the sun again was quite possibly the most uplifting feeling in the world. That warmth that bathed my face and body and the strength I felt.

That moment pales in comparison to those two words.

"Good." It's all I can say. What else is there to say? What else could I offer but that? I turn back to stare out the window into the darkness and breath a slow breath of relief.

They're safe.

"When this is over?"

She smiles at my words, said in a voice that I haven't ever heard from my own mouth. It's shaky.

"Yeah, when this is over."

Good. More reason to deal with Zeus and his ilk as soon as possible.

In the French hills there was a stone monastery, purchased by a mysterious party and run by a lean man who dressed plainly and carried himself calmly. He had a sister, a beautiful young woman that was much loved by the local children.

Their home wasn't much of a place to look at from the outside. The view from the hilltop was stunning though and he often found himself staring out over the rolling green hills and trees and gentle villages that lay nearby.

The locals had often mused about the man, he came down infrequently to purchases food and items. They had stumbled upon him during his morning run or afternoon walks from time to time and he often carried a long, polished stave of some sort of redwood. Thin veins of black ran through the wood.

He was kind, though obviously alert.

She wandered through town more freely than he did and the locals found her to be ever curious, ever interested in learning more.

Theories abounded about the pair from the monastery, though none were close.

It wasn't until a flood had struck, when an elderly local man had become trapped in his car when a road washed out. There was no help to be found and water was rising rapidly.

A figure dashed from the tree line and waded into the rushing water, driving the stave through the violent flow and pulling himself step by painful step towards the car. For a moment it seemed as if he would be washed away too but he held his ground, almost as if the waters parted for him. Driving his elbow into the window of the car,

Apollo hefted the man out into the free air and carried him to safety on drier ground.

The legend of the man from the monastery never faded, even as the years passed by. It carried onward.

Apollo and Athena descended into folklore of the area, though no one spoke of the triplets that lived under their watchful eyes.

They never really saw those three, intentionally so. They lived at risk should they be discovered by Zeus, for they had a power in their blood that he desired.

Apollo and Athena had secreted away Hyperion's children.

Chapter XXXI

Kronos was frustrated. Everyone could see as much, most were avoiding him. Not that it was easy in the small house.

Athena felt she had an idea for bringing back Coeus and that was the only good news he had since Hyperion disappeared. That disappeared the moment the front door flew open and Prometheus ran into the house, shouting.

"Kronos!" His feet thundered on the stairs while he continued yelling, "Kronos!"

His head stuck through the doorway of the bedroom that Kronos was hiding in, disappeared and then reappeared.

"Kronos!"

Kronos stared at him.

"Yes. It's me. What?"

"Aphrodite needs your help, I need your help. Quickly!" He disappeared again.

"What the hell is going on?" Kronos shouted after him.

"They have Atlas and Menoetius!"

Kronos lurched off the edge of the bed and raced after Prometheus, that was not good.

Aphrodite still looked well put together though Prometheus looked disheveled. He had given up on the suit jacket and reverted to a wrinkled dress shirt that was open at the neck. His crisp hair was sticking out at various angles and a shotgun rested on his chest with a strap holding it around his neck.

"Bad, bad, very bad," Prometheus was cursing as he loaded shotgun shells into the weapon, "so bad."

"What is going on?" Hades was the first to speak, following Kronos into the kitchen where Prometheus was now making a mess. A shotgun shell rolled off the table, Prometheus cursed at it and caught it when Hades tossed it back at him, not pausing his frenetic loading to say a thank you.

"Hera found two of the kids, she's had them for at least a week." Aphrodite was also calmer than Prometheus, who knocked over the whole box of ammunition and shouted more choice curses.

"Shit." Hades started loading several magazines for a pistol, standing beside Prometheus who was knocking shells with his feet and coming up with ever more inventive phrases.

"What's going on?" Rhea said it this time, expressing the confusion of all the others that had come to see the show.

"Hera, she's not the woman you knew, just know that now before I- "

"-what is going on?" Rhea repeated it.

"She's torturing two of Iapetus' children. Atlas and Menoetius. She's trying to find a way to use Titan blood for Olympians."

Rhea placed her hands on the counter to steady herself, closing her eyes and taking a long breath. Phoebe and Mnemosyne both touched an arm with concern. They had been close.

"She's a monster," Rhea hissed through clenched teeth, the house shivering with her rage as it bubbled through the foundations of the entire neighborhood. Rhea pushed down on the countertop with both hands, palms flat as the surface molded to her anger.

"It's not your fault," Aphrodite was the first to reach Rhea, placing a hand on hers. The shaking slowed and then stopped entirely as Rhea regained her composure.

When she opened her eyes again there was a hardness to them that none of the Titans had seen before, a harsh edge.

"Take us there, now."

Crius and Mnemosyne elected to stay behind, hoping to help Athena with Coeus. Apollo and Phoebe stayed with them. Prometheus drove one vehicle and Aphrodite the other, piling the remaining Titans and their counterparts into two black SUVs. Prometheus white knuckled the steering wheel as he drove, driving too fast and obviously unconcerned about it.

Kronos sat in the front seat, trying not to stare at the road as it flew by them dangerously fast.

Prometheus glanced over, his demeanor a far cry from the last time they'd met. He wasn't smiling a cocky grin or making jokes. He wasn't angry either, not like Rhea.

He was scared.

"I'd go faster if I could," he said, glancing to Kronos and then to the rear-view mirror to Hermes and Tethys, who both looked as nervous as Kronos felt. He could feel Prometheus tapping his free foot while the other pressed down on the gas pedal, sending a thumping shiver through the vehicle.

"How far is it?" Kronos asked, as they rocketed past another vehicle on the road, nearly sending the innocent driver into the ditch.

"Too far," Prometheus said, "two hours."

He looked back to the road and forced the gas pedal down even further, the engine roaring as it obliged.

"Too far."

Two security guards watched the entry gate, barely able to tear their eyes away from their magazines and the grainy television they had smuggled into the security booth. Not that their supervisor cared all that much about what they did on the night shift. Nothing happened at a research facility at night aside from a handful of research scientists working late.

So, the two guards sat and watched a show that could have easily been almost anything, the amount of fuzz made it almost impossible to know what it was.

The first had his feet up on another chair, stolen from the third guard that was new.

They had sent him on a patrol of the grounds.

"Kid tucks his goddamn pants into his boots," the older of the two grumbled again. The younger flipped to the next page of his magazine as he rolled his eyes.

"Frank, please, not again. I get it, you wish you were young again or some shit. Just, not tonight, cool?"

Frank grumbled some more and then went deathly silent. The younger flipped another page.

"Nothing more to say?"

Frank didn't respond. The young glanced up from his magazine to see Frank sitting in his chair, fully tense and pushing himself back into the chair support. Almost as if he was trying to push himself right through the chair.

That wasn't so eye-catching, it was the enormous lion of earth that had teeth bared at the older security guard. That was eye-catching. The younger guard opened his mouth to scream but a hand clamped over his face and a voice whispered in his ear.

"Quietly now, he's skittish."

Frank didn't move as the lion closed in on his face, a low rumbling emanating from its chest. He didn't even tremble.

"What do you want?" he asked of the woman who stood beside the lion.

She smiled.

A second security station was inside the building, manned by two Hoplites. They were not like the perimeter guards, they sat stone faced and with intent focus as they watched the many security cameras throughout the building. There were no magazines or TV screens, just the two unsettling men that watched the screen.

One of them saw movement on one of the many screens and leaned forward, relaxing a moment later when two of the outer guards walked into view from one of the hallways. They wore their grey hats so that the brims covered their faces, but they walked in the same slovenly manner that the Hoplites had come to expect of those guards.

The Hoplite leaned back into his chair, relaxed and with attention turned back to the many other screens.

It wasn't more than a minute or two later when he saw the movement again and again leaned forward, wondering why those two guards were coming down the hall towards their security office. He stood, walked the few steps to the door and put a hand on the handle to find out why the guards were so far from their posts.

He never managed to turn the handle. Instead the door came off its hinges and struck him in the chest, tossing him across the room and into the screens with bursts of glass and sparks flying as his body demolished a dozen of the screens. The other moved quickly, spinning in his chair and on his feet before Kronos and Hermes were inside the room. He reached for the sidearm on his thigh, but Hermes was fast too. Hermes delivered a hammer blow to the Hoplite's wrist with a sickening *crack* as bones shattered.

The Hoplite didn't even grunt in pain but engaged Hermes with his good arm, moving almost as fast as the Olympian.

Kronos had no time to step in before the second Hoplite was on his feet and coming forward in a fighting stance, not bothering with his sidearm but instead opening an extendable weapon with a flick of his wrist.

Kronos took his sickle out from the back of his pants and the Hoplite just smiled at him.

There were sparks as the two traded blows, Kronos blocking the strikes that seemed to carry an extraordinary amount of strength behind them. It was a dance, moving forward to attack and backward with the defense, though the space didn't quite allow it. Hermes and the other Hoplite were equally matched in speed. It wasn't speed that gave the Hoplite the advantage.

It was a cup of hot coffee that he'd been drinking.

He moved in a feint and Hermes responded, giving the Hoplite the opening to pick up the cup and toss the contents at Hermes' face. He dodged it, but the Hoplite followed up the dirty tactic with a heavy side kick right into Hermes' gut, driving all the air out of him and tossing him to the floor.

Kronos spared a quick glanced over but couldn't do anything. The extendable weapon was too quick for him to lose focus on it. Hermes was on the ground and a pair of incredibly strong hands were crushing his throat.

Kronos ground his teeth and ducked under an overhanded swing, bringing the sickle across in a sweeping attack that opened bloody wounds on both thighs of the Hoplite. Again, there was no sound of pain.

There was a slight slowing of the man's movements though as blood began to pump through the gashes.

The Hoplite looked up and snarled, his face curling with an animalistic rage.

Then his left eye exploded, and a gunshot echoed in the room like a clap of thunder. The Hoplite dropped to the floor, his life snuffed out. Kronos ducked and turned to see who had entered the fray.

Hades had fired the round from a pistol, but Prometheus was not so restrained. He fired his shotgun once into the chest of the Hoplite attempting to throttle Hermes, the solid round tearing through his vest and punching a gaping hole out his back. He jerked once with the impact and then limply fell onto his side. Prometheus was sure the Hoplite was dead.

He let the shotgun dangle in one hand and offered the other to Hermes, pulling Hermes to his feet with no small amount of effort. There was already bruising spreading on Hermes neck and that was concerning to Kronos.

"They're not wholly mortal," Kronos said, looking down at the bloodied body of the one he had fought.

Hades fired his pistol into the other Hoplite's head.

"They do die though," he said, "So there's that."

"Hoplites," Prometheus said, "She did it. She made them."

"*Made* them?"

Prometheus nodded, kicking at the body of the men that had put up a good fight.

"Hera wanted the Titanic children to make soldiers. Zeus wanted to be truly immortal, he wanted to be a big god in a small temple. Hera wanted to be *the* god."

Kronos watched the red blood of a mortal seep from the wounds, mixed with the black blood of Titans. They were not mortal, nor were they gods. They were dangerous.

They had to stop it.

Kronos hoped that Rhea and the others had not had any problems.

Oceanus fell to the ground, pinned by a Hoplite who hit him with a devastating flurry of blows with her fists. He blocked as best he could before striking her on the side of the head with the handle of the trident, knocking her away. He leaped to his feet and drove the three points through her chest so hard that they pierced the concrete floor beneath her body as she writhed and coughed up red blood with black spots.

Tethys stabbed her short dagger into another Hoplite, through the protective vest, dodging slow and heavy blows from the largest of the group they had encountered. The man was at least seven feet tall and still moved quickly for his size, just not as quickly as Tethys. She dove the tip into his body again and again, dodged a blow and slashed open another wound on an arm or a leg, then thrust the blade into his flesh again. He was bleeding so heavily he barely looked human anymore.

Rhea's lion clamped down on the leg of a Hoplite and it snapped, the bone break echoing in the large room they had stumbled on. Rhea was not much of a fighter. She was furious, so she waded into this fight. It was not eagerly but it was with skill.

They had entered the other side of the facility while Kronos and Hermes distracted anyone watching the cameras. Prometheus had spent six months working at the facility as an annoying, ex-military type to get an idea of what was happening at the facility.

What he did not know was that the Hoplites would gather in a room for late night training that was usually a storage area. They had opened the door to find ten Hoplites training in close quarters, drenched in sweat and carrying blunted training weapons including spears and swords.

Both groups had stared at each other for the briefest moment until the chaos erupted.

They went at each other in a desperate struggle for life, a game of tug-of-war where the stakes were life or death. It was Aphrodite that surprised most of all, stealing a long, blunted staff from one of the Hoplites and using it with deadly efficiency. She was in the middle of the fighting, she had not been trapped in a prison for three thousand years and moved like it. She tore through a handful of the Hoplites, breaking arms and legs as she went through them with ease. They were tough and tried to stand on shattered knees or attack with arms that dangled limply from broken joints or bones.

It didn't take long for it to be over, bodies strewn about the training room with shattered weapons and pools of blood spreading out from fatal wounds. The room was gruesome but all of them ignored the wheezing sounds of one or two Hoplites that were still on their way to meet death, instead looking at the blood pools.

"That's Titan blood," Rhea said, "where are they getting Titan blood from?"

"Nowhere good, we have to hurry."

Aphrodite rushed them out of the room and into a hallway, nearly running headlong into Prometheus.

"Have a problem?" he said, looking at the blood spatters on her clothes and face. She knocked him lightly with the blunted staff, tapping his upper thigh with a reasonably gentle strike. He winced and hissed at her, then led the group down a hallway towards the secretive elevator.

He turned a corner and stopped dead in his tracks, staring with a quizzical look plastered on his face. The others joined him and saw what had stopped him. Visible at the end of the hall was a polished, gleaming elevator door to their end goal. It was only fifty feet away, maybe less.

Prometheus wasn't looking at the door though.

He was looking at the shield wall that was held in place by at least a dozen Hoplites. They had blocked the hallway with perfect efficiency, each shield interlocked with the one beside it and an incredibly fit Hoplite holding each in place. The front bristled with spear tips to add danger to the defense.

"Ah, the best defense is a good offense and defense," Hades said, grinning as the others shot him glares and rolled their eyes. Kronos ignored the quip and placed both his hands on the hall to his left, closing his eyes and focusing. The building vibrated with Titanic power as he filtered his will from his mind into the concrete walls, drawing as deep as he could to find whatever energy there was.

"Hades, do you know where our power comes from?" he asked it without opening his eyes. Hades glanced at the others in the hall, no one was coming to help him on this one.

"The weapons, I assume."

Kronos opened his eye and they were entirely brown, a deep swirling color with flecks of gold and grey mixed into the terrifying image. He smiled as the vibrating stopped.

"Faith. Belief. People."

The swirling brown drained from his eyes, the power flowing from Kronos body to the concrete walls with the force of belief that had begun to return. People had begun to believe in gods again. If only a few so far but word of gods was spreading in the mortal world.

The Hoplites held their shield wall in place with the cocky arrogance of mortals that believe themselves to be close to gods, something mortals with power were always good at doing. They were not expecting the power of a Titan, a power that hadn't been seen in millennia.

The wall bowed to Kronos' will and thrust out spears of concrete through the side of the Hoplites, dozens of spikes punching through flesh and cloth and armor as if they were nothing. There was no time to scream or shout or even move, the long, thin spikes were too quick. In the blink of an eye the dozen Hoplites were skewered in the hall, blood seeping around the concrete spikes and dripping to the floor.

Kronos held his hands against the wall and the spikes withdrew, again in the blink of an eye. The Hoplites crumpled to the floor, their shield wall crumbling as the most important piece failed. The person holding the shield.

The way to the elevator was clear. So onward they went, carefully picking their way over the fresh corpses with fist sized holes marking their bodies.

Hades didn't make any smart comments.

None of the Olympians had seen a Titan's power in a very long time, they had forgotten it. If they'd ever seen it in full.

So, Hades said nothing because he had nothing to say. He watched the Titans and for a moment he felt afraid.

Iapetus sat in the back of a black SUV, his phone crunching into a useless mass as he closed his fist around it. The Colonel was a physically impressive man and now Iapetus would likely be stuck in this form for the rest of his life. Which might be shorter than he would have expected. Neither were ideal.

Hera had been confident in her "Hoplites" and Kronos had just killed a dozen of them without missing a beat, his power was growing too rapidly. Demeter had made a mistake when she thought framing the Titans for destroying a town would work. She was an idiot.

The Olympians were working against each other and crowing about how they worked together.

Idiots.

He looked at his crushed phone and thought about Hera, toying with her new pets and likely unaware that the Titans had come. Her confidence in her pet projects had driven her to remain there. Arrogance and intelligence are undesirable traits when working in tandem.

He thought about asking Ares for his phone. Then he decided against it.

She had made her choice.

Besides, he had other places to be.

They all crowded into the elevator as it descended into the depths of Hera's research facility, listening to the soft music that played in the cramped space.

"I like this song," Hades said, his sense of humor back after the display in the hall. Oceanus delivered a soft punch to his gut and Hades let out a grunt.

"Always with the violence."

At that moment the lights went out and the elevator jolted to a halt, throwing everyone inside around and into each other.

"Who am I touching?" Hades' voice echoed in the silence, followed by the ear-splitting sound of a hand striking a cheek.

"Ah, Aphrodite!"

"No, it's Prometheus, you twit, get your hands off me!"

"Prometheus? Well, you have a deceptively nice ass."

"Stop it!"

The lights came back on and Hades rubbed his cheek, where a red spot was spreading. When the elevator doors opened with a polite *ding* there was a wall of Hoplites armed with rifles, not spears. They had upgraded their arsenal for this fight.

They were ready for the doors to open and started shooting the moment they did. Kronos was first to act, raising a concrete barrier from the floor. He tensed and struggled to hold the barrier, his energy drained from the assault on the shield wall.

"A little help," he said, gritting his teeth, "soon would be good."

"Oceanus!" Tethys pointed to the nearest wall then cupped her hands, drawing out her elemental. Oceanus drove the blunt end of the trident into the concrete and began tearing chunks out. He found what he was looking for.

"Hold your breath," Tethys said. Kronos let the wall start to crumble.

On the other side, Hoplites grew confident as the wall fell apart, a dozen of them with rifles in shooting stances. There were two more behind the firing line, massive men, each carried a two-handed hammer. They approached the wall as it started to fall, raising their weapons.

They stopped in their tracks as the concrete fell apart. The wall was replaced by a surreal sight of several Titans and Olympians suspended in a block of water. They hung there, one of the smaller ones waved at them.

They turned on their heels as the water rushed down the hall. Tethys' elemental forced the water flow from the broken pipe out to sweep the Hoplites off their feet, the force breaking some ankles as they tried to fight it. Once the Hoplites were down on hands and knees in the rushing torrent of water, the elemental began to fill the hallway.

It controlled the area with the Titans, dropping the level so they could breathe again while raising the water in the hallway to the ceiling. It began to cycle the water, churning the Hoplites around and into each other and the walls. They struggled in their attempts to escape but they couldn't.

Tethys held out a hand and the churning stopped, the Hoplites struggling to their feet in the water. The elemental allowed them enough air to stay alive and just enough room to let them stand.

"Just one minute, I have to deal with something."

She stepped into the water, her elemental creating a solid barrier so none of the others could follow. Hermes tried to reach out for her, but Oceanus grabbed his hand.

"Let her do this boy, just watch."

Hermes did watch.

Tethys moved as if she wasn't encased in water, her elemental buoyed her movements and allowed her to run as if on dry land. She was graceful as she did so, even if they hadn't been slowed in the water the Hoplites would have almost been standing still to it.

She was mad.

She dropped to her knees as the two massive Hoplites slowly swung their hammers in a wide sweeping arc at her chest. She slid under both swings and slashed out with her dagger. She targeted one of the massive men first, slicing from his ankle and up the back of his calf, all the way to his upper thigh. She stabbed it into the side of his stomach twice, three times, four times, moving up his body with each thrust. She kicked the back of his knee and the Hoplite dropped to one knee. She gripped his chin and slid the knife across his throat.

All had happened in no more than a few seconds, leaving his body suspended in the water as blood darkened her elemental. Those with firearms tried to shoot at her but their bullets just exploded in the water harmlessly. They were too slow to help the second large Hoplite. Tethys leaped through the water and drove her dagger into his eye. He fell backwards in slow motion while Tethys moved off him, seemingly flying through the water at the rest of the Hoplites.

Hermes lost sight of her in the cloud of red that darkened the water. They all waited, watched for any sign of movement. They could hear nothing through the water, a few muffled gunshots were all they could make it.

Without warning the water collapsed, draining out under doors and through gaps to reveal Tethys and more than a dozen Hoplite corpses. She breathed in, slowly and evenly and looked to the other as water dripped from her hair. In one hand was the dagger and the other her elemental as an orb of controlled water. She sheathed her dagger and started wringing out her long hair that was plastered to her face and scalp.

"Shall we?" she tilted her head towards the next door. Prometheus stepped over the bodies in the hall.

"Why did you guys go up against them?" he whispered to Hermes. Hermes chewed on his lower lip nervously before he answered.

"We fucked up."

"Yeah, I figured that part out all by myself," Prometheus said it as he stepped over one of the large Hoplites, with a very disgusting eye wound. When the Hoplite suddenly reached out and grabbed his ankle in an iron grip, Prometheus yelped. Then he dropped the barrel of his shotgun right against the Hoplite's forehead and squeezed the trigger twice.

The twin blasts made an absolute mess all over the corridor.

"I sure hope he's dead," Hades said, lifting his very fine shoes up as the spreading pool reached out for them, before giving up and stepping through the blood gingerly. He muttered something about how expensive the shoes were as he did.

"Let's get this over with before you all ruin something else of mine," he said, leading them to the door and pushing it open. Beyond the door was a series of airlock doors, accessible only by a pass card. Prometheus had thought to take one weeks earlier and it still worked, allowing the group to pass into a large room with multiple workstations and large pieces of equipment.

Hera sat in the center of the room on a wheeled chair, one leg crossed over the other and a general look of distaste at the intruders.

"I see you let yourselves in," she said dryly, "I wish you hadn't."

Rhea stormed towards her old friend, feet thundering on the floor and her lion plodding beside heavily, a deep growl rumbling through its chest.

Hera stood, smoothed her white lab coat and held up her hands. Rhea closed the gap and stood bare inches from Hera's face.

"You'll not want to make any hasty decisions," she said, her voice steady, "we have so much to talk about."

"Rhea…" Kronos said it, his voice shook as he did, something that was rare in her usually unflappable brother. She left her lion growling, watching Hera and turned to see what had drawn her brother's attention. Oceanus was grinding his jaw so intently that she could hear it across the room. Tethys had her head buried in Hermes' shoulder and was heaving with tearful sobs. Aphrodite was trying to make a desperate call out on her cellphone.

It was no use, they were too deep underground.

"We have *so* much to talk about," Hera repeated. Rhea hit her across the mouth with a closed fist, sending the woman sprawling to the floor with a grunt.

Kronos didn't rush to stop her, he just slowly walked towards a large cylindrical tank. It was filled with a bluish tinted water, cables and wires and tubes spreading out from the cylinder and into dozens of screens and computers on the outside. Beside it were two smaller tanks with bodies suspended inside them as well. One was a very large man with wild eyes that was staring at Prometheus. His breath bubbled from around a clear tube that was shoved down his throat.

"Atlas," Prometheus breathed out, rushing to the tanks with Aphrodite close behind. The other was Menoetius, who was unconscious.

In the center of the three tanks was a body, suspended in the liquid and hanging limply from several supporting straps and devices.

It was a face all the Titans recognized.

It was Iapetus.

I was held in place, helpless and unable to move while Themis was pierced by a blade. Over and over again it tore into her flesh. She opened her mouth and black blood poured out, coating the front of her shirt. She tried to choke out words through all the blood. Nothing came out. Just more blood.

Theia looked at me with pleading eyes, calling out for me.

"Please, help me, please!" she begged, as scalpels and knives parted her flesh. More blood. She screamed for relief, for help but none came. I was helpless.

Iapetus looked at me with his eyes, weakness coursing through his body as the world forgot about him. He tilted his head back and blood drained from the gruesome cut along his neck.

I screamed in my helplessness, struggling against the bonds to help my siblings. To get to them, to stop the pain and suffering. I could do nothing.

I opened my eyes slowly, listening to the tires rumble against the roadway. We were on a highway and there were plenty of headlights passing by us, both from behind and in front. Artemis had explained that she had to drive with moderate caution or we would have to explain to a completely innocent police officer why we had a gigantic three-headed dog in the back of the car.

I grumbled about it, even if she wasn't wrong. I had taken the chance to sleep. It wasn't like I needed much but it did help freshen the mind and I hadn't slept in days.

That's when the dreams had started.

I rubbed my eyes and forced back the tears, Artemis watching me from the corner of her eye.

"You alright?"

I shook my head. She didn't press the issue.

I couldn't get them out of my head, their faces were plaguing me. Theia, Themis, Iapetus.

Iapetus.

I furrowed my eyebrows and thought back to the prison. He had been right beside me when we started for the hangar. I remember that. He was with me step by step until he just wasn't. How did they get him without me noticing?

"How…" I said it out loud and Artemis looked at me with questions in her eyes. I thought of my brother's eyes and the depths that lived behind them.

"Faith." I mumbled, thinking back the mountain and the war that raged below. His eyes, he had looked to the war below in the moment that we were banished to Tartarus. He had been sad.

"It was never faith…" I looked up at her and panic settled in my chest.

"What are you talking about?"

"Coeus said he couldn't remember and couldn't forget. He figured it out. He figured it out and they destroyed his mind. Gods be damned I'm an idiot," I said, slamming my hands on the dashboard of the van so hard it bent under the impact. Cerberus looked at me and whined deep in his throats and Artemis was clearly confused.

"Turn around, turn around now!" I shouted, "we need to get back to them. They're in danger."

She turned the wheel so hard I thought the whole thing would overturn. Other drivers honked and cursed at us as we spun across the lanes and Artemis pointed us in the other direction.

"What the hell is going on?" she said, calmly dodging the angry drivers and crossing the earthen divider between each roadway.

"It's Iapetus, he's not dead. And he can find Coeus."

"Shit," she breathed out, looking at the clock, "Hyperion…it's been hours. We won't make it."

"We have to."

I closed my eyes and listened to the engine roar as she pressed her foot down, our speed gaining. I hadn't done it in thousands of years, but I found my lips moving before I could think about what I was doing.

"Father, we need help. Please."

I couldn't have known but Phoebe suddenly went stiff, all those miles away from me. She heard it. Felt it.

"They're coming!"

Chapter XXXII

The door burst inwards under the heavy boot of The Colonel, still being possessed by Iapetus. He was furious, since he knew that his real body was lost. Unless they could win.

The men rushed into the house with weapons up.

Athena stood between Phoebe and Coeus, guarding the door. Jeff was armed with a pistol and watching his wife and children, weakened by his broken ribs. Apollo and Crius were on the lower level of the house awaiting their prey. The men moved quickly into each room, sweeping for targets. Four entered the living room while another four moved through the kitchen and dining room. Four more headed for the stairs to check the second level. Iapetus moved with those four, sure that they would be hiding on the second level.

In the living room, one of the men placed a hand on a closet door knob and waited for the nod from the group leader. With the nod he yanked open the door to reveal nothing more than some hanging clothes and a vacuum. They turned to see that Apollo now stood in the doorway to the living room, holding a long spear.

There was a long pause, a careful consideration of the chances.

Then one of them tried to raise his rifle and fire.

Apollo spun the spear and moved behind it, as if dancing. The blur of motion disguised where he was, his movements too quick to track. When he closed the gap, he thrust the spear through the neck of the first Hoplite. Then the battle began. The three still living opened fire and shredded furniture, walls and everything but Apollo.

Crius sat in the kitchen, dancing a small knife across his fingers. One leg bounced with barely contained energy as the four-man team entered the kitchen. Crius was up from the chair in a heartbeat, sliding across the smooth floor on his knees and slashing the knife in a wide arc. It severed flesh and muscle as it swept through the legs of the first two men. The next two men began firing their weapons.

Outside, muzzle flashes lit up the windows of the dining room, followed by shouting before a body crashed through the large glass window and came to rest on the grass. Then the night was still again.

Apollo and Crius quickly mounted the stairs, taking them three at a time to the upper level. A door opened, and he turned to see The Colonel with a pistol held to the head of a little girl with blonde hair. The Colonel raised the pistol as Crius threw his knife, an underhand throw with the point. A shot sounded but Crius was already moving, sliding down the hall floor and tackling The Colonel against a wall. He grabbed the man's arm and slammed it against the bedroom wall again and again until the pistol clattered away into the hallway.

The Colonel delivered a striking knee blow to Crius' stomach, doubling him over. He slammed a fist across the young Titan's cheek, dropping him to the floor. The Colonel kicked the door shut and heaved a small chair through the nearest window.

He paused in the window frame as Crius managed to get to his feet.

"Goodbye, little brother."

Crius' stopped for the span of a blink at the words.

The Colonel stepped backwards and as he dropped to the lawn below. From a house across the street Ares squeezed the trigger of his rifle. The Titanic bullet hit Crius in the center of his chest and the youngest Titan grunted as he came to a stop, holding a hand up to the blood pumping from the hole that had suddenly appeared. Apollo was through the door and caught him just before Crius slumped to the floor. He held the youngest Titan in his arms and looked to Athena.

She tore Crius' shirt open to see the wound, as black veins spread out from the bullet hole. Crius gasped for air and started to shake, trying to speak as the blood filled his lungs and his body failed.

"I...I...I..."

Athena shook her head and Apollo cradled Crius, hushing him. Phoebe ran to her brother and held his hand, while Coues stood behind them, staring down at his little brother.

They heard the boots on the main level, more coming up the stairs. The girls held their mother while Apollo held Crius, no one able to move as the Titan slowly stopped moving and breathing. As Crius died.

Coeus stood in the doorway and his eyes flashed a bright green. There were tears in his eyes as he closed the door before anyone could move. Athena tried to go for the door, but Phoebe held her back, shaking her head. Her brother was back.

Coeus picked the pistol from the floor and swiftly checked it. The first man to come up the stairs found himself staring down the barrel before the bullet entered his eye and he saw no more. As he fell backward Coeus ripped a rifle out of the man's hands and kicked his body into the men on the stairs. They stumbled as the body fell and looked up to Coeus, who emptied the rifle into the packed group of men. He calmly walked down the steps among the bodies, shooting two more men that came through the front door.

He had heard at least one more. He closed his eyes and listened.

He heard the footsteps, a soft crunch of boots on soft earth and blades of grass. He lifted the pistol and fired one shot, rewarded with a heavy thud as the last mercenary fell with a bullet lodged in his back.

Coeus found them still in the bedroom. He tossed the pistol away and held Phoebe as she launched herself into his arms, weeping into his shoulder.

"We have to leave."

Athena nodded, and Apollo went to pick up Crius' body. Coeus stopped him.

"I'll carry him."

He knelt beside his little brother, the one he had always felt closest to. The curious little brother, the exploratory mind. They had been so alike in that way. He kissed Crius' forehead lightly before he lifted the Titan's body.

Gently and carefully, Coeus carried his little brother out of the house while tires screamed to a halt in front of the house. Hyperion stepped out.

"You figured it out," Coeus said it quietly, laying Crius to the grass. "But not fast enough."

I stared down at the body for a long time, feeling the crushing weight of my own failures and decisions on my shoulders. Our little brother, with his good heart and curious mind was gone. Another one stolen from us.

"It's Iapetus," I finally said, the pain of the words like a dagger through my soul.

"It is. Our brother seeks power, as these false gods do. He is lost to us."

Coeus' eyes are his own and I see the depths of sadness and knowledge in them as he looks at me, into my soul. I see my pain reflected in them.

"It's good to know you're not lost," I say. He tilts his head at me and his eyes look down to Crius.

"I still feel lost," he says in reply.

When the others come they find us sitting there, saying our goodbye in our own way. Coeus hums a very old song that I haven't heard in a few thousand years and strokes Crius' hair. There is a heavy silence while Prometheus and Aphrodite take two men that I do not know into the house. Kronos and the others sit on the grass with us, Hades takes a position with Crius and grinds his jaw with blinding rage that I can feel in the air.

The sun rises as the night is driven away and I feel the surging power in my fingertips, a crackling energy that flows through my body. I flex my hands and wonder why it feels so different, so much more like it did in the old days.

"They believe again, not many but enough," Kronos says.

If only it had come sooner. Maybe we'd have avoided all of this.

Maybe not.

We'll never know the truth of that. And going back in time is something none of us can do. Time is beyond any god.

I look up as the door to the house opens and Jeff steps out, bleary eyed and chewing his bottom lip. I don't blame the mortal, he's now lived through an all-out assault. And they had his daughter from what I hear. I'd be nervous in his shoes too.

Look at me, understanding mortal qualms.

I see his daughter peeking from the doorway, her mother with her, looking almost as bad as Jeff does. And suddenly I feel a surge of something else through my body, matching the intensity of the power that I gather from the sun.

I will protect these mortals. I blink and feel a crushing weight in my chest, as if the magnitude of that thought becomes real and solid in my body.

I feel a hand on my shoulder and Coeus looks down at me with a sad smile.

"Finally," he says.

"Hyperion," Jeff comes closer to us, clearing his throat and trying to keep the tears in his eyes from coming. I understand that he and Crius were becoming close. I stand and look Jeff in the eyes until he holds out a phone, I take it and hold it up to my ear.

"I didn't want Crius to die, but you left me no choice."

I recognize the voice. The cadence is Iapetus, but the tone is The Colonel, a man I should have killed in Tartarus.

"Why?" is all I can ask, hearing my own voice break even with just the single word.

"Let us finish this, you and me. Where it began. Just you and me."

A mortal word appears in my mind, flashing in red. I had heard it only a few times, but I enjoyed it.

Bullshit. He was lying.

I flexed my hands and thought about the change I had felt, not to mention the seething rage that coursed through my veins. It was like fire in my blood and it felt good. If only it didn't feel so horrendous to have been betrayed by everyone we once trusted. Even our brother.

"You think I'm lying, that's fine…" he says to me, his voice wrong coming from his prisoner. I hadn't thought it possible. Who would have? A god living inside a mortal form, it's wrong.

"-but, if you do this I will help you bring back Theia, Crius, Themis. All of them."

My breath caught in my throat. He was a Titan of life and death. This claim was not out of the realm of his abilities.

"We can rule together, like the old days. Mortals kneeling to us, bowing to us, dying for us. Remember the thrill of battle? Of real war? It can be ours again. These Olympians have used up their value. Let us take our place again."

I remember the fire and smoke and the blood and the ring of metal on metal as hundreds of thousands of mortals died for us. I remember the edge of pleasure that it brought me, the fire and blood. They were everything to me.

And our brothers and sisters returned to us. Our place as rulers made concrete.

"I will come. Alone."

The call ends. Even across all this distance I can feel him smiling. I wonder if he knows what's coming.

I'm not sure if I know what's coming yet.

I look at Jeff and wonder if I can ask what I am about to ask of him.

"I need a pilot."

He shrugs his shoulder and a duffel bag hits the grass with a wet thud and he smiles at me.

"I'm already packed."

"You're doing what?" Kronos didn't yell the words and that was more unsettling than if he'd gone into a furious rage.

"He asked me to come to him at Tartarus, alone."

"And you are going to do it?"

"Yes."

He stares at me. For a long time.

"Are you sure about this?" he asks. I shake my head at him. How could I possibly be sure? He seems to understand though.

"I want you to come, you and Rhea. Just in case."

"That's not alone."

"I have a plan, but it only works if there's just a few of us. And I'll need you in the end."

He raises an eyebrow at me. Probably because I used the word "plan" and that's not something I've ever said before.

"Alright. I trust you."

I can't help the smile that tugs at the corner of my mouth. He'd never said that before. Not once.

"Don't say anything, you'll ruin it." He says.

But it's too late.

It's already ruined.

Chapter XXXIII

Ares sat behind the desk and seethed in a deep rage. He was being called to answer for resources that had become known to the United States government, misdirection of funds and personnel. They wanted answers and they wanted blood.

His blood.

Subordinate officers had deserted him in droves, once information started to filter in about what was coming down there were only two options for them.

Career suicide or become a sprinter to get away from the mess.

They chose to sprint.

Ares was not well liked in the community. He couldn't retain any security personnel and the private community had blacklisted him. Word spread that scores of men and women had died for the six-figure salary being offered by Ares and it did not look good.

He had called an old friend and that friend had laughed him off, told him that it was more lucrative and far safer to do personal security for whichever up and coming fifteen-year-old starlet needed it.

When his office door opened Ares opened his mouth to scream obscenities at whoever was interrupting his breakdown when he looked up to see a familiar face.

Hades wore his suit jacket open, a bright red tie against a pristine white shirt. He sat in the chair opposite Ares who didn't have the wherewithal to say anything. He just sat and fumed, holding the phone in one hand and the other resting on the desk.

"Having trouble?" Hades picked at some unseen speck of dirt under a fingernail, a smirk plastered on his face. His jacket lay open and Ares saw the handle of a dagger, a dagger he recognized.

"Look, it wasn't my- "

"Shut up." Hades said. He sighed heavily and rolled his eyes, "You didn't do anything you didn't want to do. You were always a loudmouth bully that thought you could just force your way through anything."

"Hyperion isn't any different!" Ares raised his voice, dropping his phone onto the desk, "bull in a china shop."

"Oh, fuck off," Hades said, brushing something off his jacket shoulder.

Ares ground his jaw and thought about the handgun in the second drawer of his desk, loaded with bullets that could kill a Titan. His eyes flicked down to the drawer.

Hades arched an eyebrow.

"Go for it big guy," he nodded his head at the drawer, "let's dance."

Tethys listened to the gunfire, perched on the desk of the military aide that sat in his chair and kept his mouth shut. The aide knew better than that. Hermes, or his alter ego, had a reputation among those types. An excellent reputation, one that had allowed Hermes, Hades and Tethys into a secure facility without so much as a second glance.

It didn't help Ares that certain elements in the government no longer thought he was worth protecting. It would be best if Ares just disappeared.

Hades was more than willing to assist in that matter, in fact he had made a few calls to ensure it fell to him. His underworld wasn't confined to actions that were entirely criminal and certain organizations had relied on him before.

Thus, they relied on him again for this.

The gunfire rattled, shaking the office. The aide's eyes darted furtively to the closed door as the shooting suddenly stopped.

"Don't worry about it," Tethys said, kicking her feet idly from her perch on the desk, "you'll be fine."

The aide was less staring at her and more at the water that moved over her fingers in a delicate dance. It wasn't possible.

The office door opened and the man with the red tie stepped out. He paused, closed the door behind him, straightened his jacket and smoothed his crumpled tie. There were flecks of blood on his white dress shirt and a few scrapes and wounds on his face and forearms.

Hades deftly flipped the dagger around and offered the hilt to the Tethys, she took it without a word and sheathed it.

"Thank you," the man in the red tie said, smiling at the aide. "He asked not to be disturbed. Perhaps you should take the night off."

The aide swallowed hard and nodded, slowly rising from his seat and taking his uniform jacket from the back of the chair. He left them there, outside the office, and hurried out of the building.

"Good?" Tethys asked of Hades.

Hades looked at her and to the office door.

"Not even close."

Chapter XXXIV

Jeff's knuckles are white, his breath is uneven. He's nervous. Hades had provided us with transport before disappearing on his own mission with Tethys and Hermes.

"Me too," I say quietly, trying to calm him. It doesn't work. Not for him and not for me.

He nods and swallows. Hard.

I like him.

"Don't..." he says as I open the door to go to whatever fate might wait in Tartarus. He stops when I look back, winces as if the words pain him, then continues.

"Don't give up on us."

I don't say anything to him. What could I say to that? Mortals asking for favors is something I am used to, they used to pray and beg for the slightest favor of any god. He wasn't asking for a favor though. He wasn't asking it of a god either.

I put a hand on him and try to give him some solace, that I won't.

I can't say it though.

I can't lie to him.

Instead I don't say anything. I just leave him there, where he'll wait to find out what the answer was.

And I find myself stepping into what might be the largest decision in the life of a god.

I stand alone in the hangar that we had escaped from so long ago. It feels like another three thousand years have passed. The reality is that it's only been two months, by the mortal timekeeping of course.

I see the blood stain from where Iapetus' body had lain while we fled, all a charade. He still controls The Colonel. His true body is beside me in a container of some kind. Hera said it helped keep his body alive, pumping blood and allowing the healing process to work.

Zeus stands to one side of Iapetus, Demeter to the other.

"What mighty gods," I say, "all three of you."

None of them smile. I thought it was clever.

Apparently, I was mistaken.

As I often am.

"You came alone?" he asks me. His voice seems wrong coming from the bald man that I despise with every fiber of my being. The cadence is right though.

"Aside from the pilot."

"Good." He seems satisfied.

"You'll bring them back?" I ask him, ignoring the other two, "you can promise me that?"

"I'll bring them back and then some, we'll be gods again. Real power, Hyperion, remember what it felt like?"

I do. I rub a thumb against the black metal chain and think back to those days. The raging battles and the thrill of hot blood and violence.

"What else?"

I know there's a price. We are gods and there is always a price to pay.

"I want my body and your word. Give me the chain and I'll know you can be trusted."

I stare at my brother in this strange body making such a demand. And I laugh. I laugh for a good thirty seconds until there are tears in the corners of my eyes. When I can breathe again I realize he meant that.

"You're serious?"

He nods. I look to the chain, the source of so much power. I couldn't possibly hand it over. Not to them.

"Think about Theia." Zeus speaks for the first time and my chest tightens. My heart beats a little harder with the mention of her name. She could be back with me.

"I am."

That's all I can manage.

I see Iapetus, in this filthy form, tilt his head at me curiously. As if he can see what I'm thinking. When he speaks it is to me and me alone. As if the others aren't there.

"All those years did change you, didn't they?"

"They did," I say, walking slowly towards him, ever cautious, "for the better I think."

He laughs.

I hold out the chain, feeling the weight of it in my hands and the power that could be unleashed by Zeus and Iapetus with my chain in their control. The power of the sun and fire. Of death.

"For Theia," I say, tossing the chain at Zeus. He greedily snatches it from the air and clutches at it, his hands running over the links like a boy with a new toy. As if he will unlock a secret by touching each link. As if the power will be his. I take a few more steps toward the three of them, Demeter looking over Zeus' shoulder at the black metal links.

Iapetus looks at me and his eyes narrow. He doesn't trust me.

"What a waste of raw talent, you were the killer I dreamed I could be." He says. If only he knew.

"We'll see."

I'm halfway to the three of them when the words slip out of my mouth. I hadn't meant to say it, it was supposed to be a thought. Expressing it so early was a mistake.

It does bring some excitement to the showdown I suppose.

There's three of them and just one of me. Well. That's what it looks like.

I force my concentration and will into the links that Zeus clutches, there is no slow orange glow or vibration or any sign at all. That would be too obvious. If only he was smarter.

Iapetus shouts a warning, Demeter moves quickly and snatches the chain from Zeus.

A lot of things happen in the next heartbeat.

Phoebe's veil drops, Kronos and Cerberus charge the gap between them and Iapetus. It's a long run, even for a Titan.

Demeter begins to throw the chain away, fearing what will come.

Zeus removes a lightning bolt from somewhere, gripping it tight and moving into a thrower's stance.

Iapetus takes one step back and I take great comfort in that. It means he is afraid.

In the next heartbeat the chain explodes. The black metals links become deadly shrapnel as all the will of the sun rushes out in a blinding white flash. Demeter is unlucky. The pieces pierce her eyes and she screams, clutching at the ragged masses that will never be whole again. Her face is raked by dozens more shards, leaving bloody furrows through her skin. Still more sink into her chest and stomach, her thighs and calves. She looks like a horrific pincushion of blood and torn flesh, falling to the hangar floor and writhing in searing pain. She takes the worst of it, blocking most of the shards from Zeus or Iapetus.

Iapetus blinks, blinded by the flash of light. Zeus as well. I charge, hoping for the best. It's my style.

There is no time to slow and I hit Zeus with a tackle, driving my shoulder into his chest with a rewarding *snap* as his ribs collapse. He grunts and we both tumble to the ground together.

We both struggle to our feet and step away from each other. He bleeds profusely from a ragged chunk of flesh that was torn from his cheek by the explosion. He also looks…afraid.

"Hyperion!"

Kronos throws something into the air at me. I catch it with one hand and let the familiar feel of warm metal rush into my body. I trust that he and Cerberus are handling Iapetus, if he chooses to fight. I have my own problem to deal with.

Zeus hits me in the stomach, driving both fists into my gut. All the air leaves my body and I grunt. I hit him back, down and across the face. I would never give up my chain and with it wrapped around my fist it hits him like a hammer on soft steel.

I hear teeth break and his jaw *pop* with the hit. He stumbles back but comes at me again, growling through the blood. He goes high, feinting with a punch so that he can drive his elbow into my shoulder.

It doesn't work. I catch his forearm and use his own momentum to toss him down. I don't let go of his arm though, letting his weight do most of the work and using my free hand to do the rest.

His forearm breaks.

A wild shriek distracts me, a weight hitting my back with ferocious intensity. Demeter can't see but she pummels my head and neck with her free hand, bites me with wild abandon and shrieks between all of that. The most damage is to my hearing, especially when Cerberus clamps three powerful jaws over her body.

Her shrieks become no less wild until they suddenly stop. Cerberus throws her limp form away and it hits the hangar floor with a disgusting slapping noise of wet flesh.

So dies Demeter.

So dies a false god.

I turn to face Zeus again. I see a crackling lightning bolt that he has hurled at me, one of The Smith's works. There is barely the span of a breath to react and it is not my reaction that saves me.

It is Cerberus. I am thrown away by an explosion of light that washes over the hangar. I find myself staring at the ceiling and wondering when the noise stopped, only to slowly recall an explosion so loud that my hearing has gone. I roll to my side and see the both Kronos and Iapetus were also thrown away by the bolt. I roll to the other side to see Cerberus. He lies still, his three heads limply piled on the floor and a wave of smoke rising from heavily burned flesh on his haunch. I feel a crushing sadness that he died for all of this. Sadness quickly becomes a burning rage.

Then I am on my feet, the ringing in my ears beginning as the world comes back to me in a crashing wave of sound and pain.

I force myself to action through the pain, I cannot fall now. The ringing gives way to someone letting out a primal roar of rage.

Then I realize it is me.

A weight hits me around the waist and I am sent flying backwards, my back hitting the floor again. Zeus is on me, fists moving in a flurry of motion at my face. His blows hit like hammers on my forearms. Pain lances through my body and I feel a bone break. I try to draw fire to me to throw him off. He slips my defense and I see stars as a fist hits my cheek. The fire doesn't come.

He stands up, looking down at me. It infuriates me how pleased he looks with himself. Even as he draws ragged breaths, he looks smug.

Maybe he should be.

He is winning.

Kronos and Iapetus are too busy struggling to their own fight to come to my aid. Phoebe is drained from the use of a veil. I am alone. He picks up my chain from the floor, swinging one end of it and taking his first steps towards me.

He is speaking but I can't hear him through the shrill sound in my ears. Gloating, I expect.

I'm glad I can't hear him.

I look over to Kronos and we have only a moment. I mouth 'sorry' to him. I heave myself up onto bruised elbows, then to my knees. I will not die on the floor. I will die standing.

I am barely to my feet when the weight of my own chain hits me, locking into place around my neck. I grip it with both hands, but it isn't mine anymore. I feel none of the energy. It is simply metal to me now.

If Zeus holds it, the power is his.

I take a stumbling step towards him, snarling my defiance even as the edges of my vision fade. I see the faces of my siblings. Theia, Themis, Crius. I will see them again.

Soon.

I fall to one knee. I have a fleeting thought that I will die on my knees. That bothers me more than anything else.

He leans down and whispers into my ear.

"It's my world now. You lose."

I begin to slip away into the darkness.

Until a blurry shape hits Zeus with all the force of a thousand gods. The chain loosens instantly, and I gasp in precious air to drive the darkness away. Zeus rolls on the floor with his attacker, who is screaming at the top of his lungs.

"It's not yours to take!" He shouts. And I watch, with ever swelling pride, as Jeff headbutts Zeus with every ounce of his strength. Zeus is stunned for a moment but not long, before I can rise to my feet again he strikes Jeff in the ribs. I hear the crack of bone and Jeff tries to scream in pain. It is a horrific gasp.

I see Zeus, there will be no surprise attack. I have the chain, there will be no weapon in his hands. He scrambles away but I am on my feet again and he has nothing.

"I am the Titan Hyperion!" I shout at him, my steps becoming steadier.

"I am the god of the sun, of rage, and I am eternal!" I lash out with the chain and fire courses through the links, breaking his leg as it hits. I lift him from the ground and ignore his begging, his pleading, his fear.

"I am the cleansing purity of fire and you are a shadow to be banished!" I wrap the chain around his throat and in one swift movement I move behind him, pulling the chain down so that his back is against mine. Both my hands pull on the links, ever closer to the floor while he chokes and sputters and thrashes against me.

Their faces flash in front of my eyes.

Theia.

Crius.

Themis.

Even Iapetus. For he is dead. Whoever he is now is not our brother.

I pull the chain down more, tighter against his neck. His struggle weakens. He is dying.

I hold their faces in my mind and I tighten my grip, pull harder.

Theia.

Crius.

Themis.

I scream their names and the chain begins to glow. From a dull orange to a bright red to a blinding white, it lights the entire hangar. I heave once, pushing up against his back while jerking my hands towards the floor. There is a thunderclap in the space as Zeus breaks.

He stops moving.

The light fades from white to red, then to orange, and finally to nothing.

Zeus is dead.

I let his body fall unceremoniously to the floor.

There is but one task at hand. Phoebe will help Jeff and see to Cerberus' body.

Kronos holds Iapetus, the real Iapetus. The Colonel, for all his former bluster, lies on the floor and whimpers. I feel a moment of pity for the man who had a Titan living in his mind and body for so long. It is a fleeting moment but a moment nonetheless. Perhaps he will be spared, along with Hera, to serve a fitting punishment.

A concern for another time.

The only concern for this time is what we will do with our brother, with our betrayer.

He looks to Jeff, our mortal ally, with all his wounds and in obvious pain. Iapetus smiles though his eyes don't.

"Furious and proud," he says quietly to me.

"They deserve better than you," I say to him, "perhaps we will be able to make it up to them. Without you."

"Then kill me." He says and when I look him in the eyes I see that he is ready for that. Kronos flinches ever so slightly. I cannot be sure, but I think he would stand against me if I tried.

"That wouldn't be justice, brother." I say.

I don't take pleasure in the confusion in my brother's eyes. I don't take pleasure in the pain we will visit on him.

One cannot take pleasure in justice.

That is what vengeance is for.

Tartarus feels different now, it had been home for so long that it almost felt natural. Now it is just a house of memories of a better time, before all this. Before I started a war and before everything went wrong. Here it began and here it ends.

This is the end of it. Our story against the gods who stole our lives from us. They had lied, they had left us to rot and they had become greed-soaked gods of their own private world.

No more.

I hold him by the shoulder and try my best not to strangle him right here, right now.

"Why?"

I ask him as he lays there, thrown into the cell by his brothers. As if we could possibly be blood after all this. He is no blood of ours.

"Because I wanted more."

My body deflates with the words. Something so simple to have sparked all of this.

"You are no brother of mine."

He stands, weakly. His body is still recovering from the grievous wound that he'd inflicted on himself. I have a hard time feeling sorry for him.

"I'm sorry Hyperion. I am sorry."

I don't speak to him, I leave him behind in that cell and I shut the door. He pulls at the chains around his ankles, the ones I recovered from the medical bay where Theia's body had been. It seemed fitting. I had strapped them to his ankles and chained him to the back wall.

He screams and pulls and begs and threatens me.

I stop and look at him.

"Take your punishment with grace, it's better than you deserve."

I toss the key at him and his eyes light up as it slides across the floor to his outstretched hands.

When he looks up he will only see the door closing and with it the ending of his life. We leave him nothing in the cell. He left us with nothing for three thousand years. We will leave him with less and for more.

I can hear his hands pounding on the inside of the heavy door, furious rage pouring through his body. He wishes for a quick death or freedom, as most of us do.

That's not justice. I learned that from my sister.

There is nothing for him inside that cell. He will share it with none. He will be alone.

There will be no one to come for him in three thousand years.

I leave Tartarus behind. Everything they had built, everything we had built for ourselves. I leave it all behind. There is nothing here for any of us now.

Kronos is the only one that waits for me.

We don't speak. There is no need. He simply brings the earth down. The medical facility that Zeus and his conspirators had constructed collapses slowly onto itself. The mountain becomes whole again. Except for a single cell, deep within the bowels. A black hole with a single occupant. Even as the mountain groans in protest as rock collapses down I think I can hear his screams from somewhere beneath all of it.

We leave our past behind us, perhaps better and perhaps not.

That doesn't matter now.

He will not die in that black pit. But he will not live either. Tartarus is sealed.

It is over.

Chapter XXXV

We gather in the yard of the house that Aphrodite had allowed us to use, a silence hanging in the air. It's a contended silence, for the first time, even though we each mourn our losses in that silence.

Someone starts a small fire and then there is beer and things go the way they often will when those things occur.

Cerberus lounges at the edge of the group, nursing his gruesome wounds and enjoying the attention that is heaped on him. I wonder if he will be remembered as the real hero of our standoff with the Olympians. I pour some of my own beer out and he laps at it, two of the three heads lolling their tongues at me in a pleased gesture.

Aphrodite lays down a package of steaks and he forgets all about me. I accept this.

Prometheus introduces the group to Atlas and Menoetius and we immediately like them. They're handsome young men with bright smiles and a nearly endless supply of humor. There's something comforting in that.

Aphrodite sits and enjoys the peace, though something behind her eyes suggests even she doesn't think it will last. She has lived in this world while we sat in our cells. She would know if there was trouble to come.

That's a problem for the future, not for now.

We find ourselves without direction for the first time in eternity, in a world that doesn't need us in many ways but in others has never been in such desperate need of gods. As night draws on us in a world without Zeus and many of the Olympians, we find ourselves gathered around a fire and thinking of everything that has happened to us. Because of us.

There have been many deaths. The mortals have begun to wonder what this means, if this is all a hoax or if there are truly gods among them. There is a great deal to take in for them and I wonder what it will mean for us.

I push the dark thoughts away and look up at the clear sky. I hope that I've made them proud. I hope that Theia is somewhere, perhaps with our father, looking on with pride. Maybe she's just gone.

We may never know.

Jeff and his family are with us. They are resilient, even after Crius' death. His girls are in love with Cerberus and since he seems to like me, they have decided I am worthy of their attention as well. They also put a braid in Oceanus' beard.

I find this amusing, though wisely I keep it to myself.

There is gentle conversation between all until I stand from my seat. I raise my drink towards Jeff.

"The mortal who tackled a god!" I say, and everyone raises their drink to Jeff. He shifts uncomfortably, as any mortal might. Hades stands as well and we both walk to Jeff. Hades carries a small bundle wrapped in purple cloth. He drops to a knee and offers it to Jeff, who places his drink in the grass and removes the cloth.

It's a simple bronze helmet with a pointed crest.

"Do you believe in gods?" I ask him quietly, while he cautiously touches the surface of the helmet.

He nods, slowly.

"I require a second!" I say. Every Titan stands. I nod my thanks to each of them, one by one. We were all in agreement on this. I also drop to a knee, joined by the others.

"This was Crius' helm. Now it falls to you, a mortal. The mortal who challenged a god. A mortal who believes, truly believes. From this night you and yours will be protected by the Titans. You will be of us, a brother. Will you accept this?"

He looks to his wife and she smiles at him, very slightly. I snort a laugh and he glares at me, breaking the solemn moment. It is done.

The stars shine brightly in the night and I can feel Crius among us, the youngest Titan with his inexhaustible naiveté. We needed him to remind to hope and to explore. Now we will do so in his memory.

We rise, Hades takes a seat beside Jeff. As I return to my seat I hear a soft thud of a fist and a whimper from Jeff.

"You challenged a god?" I hear his wife hiss. There is a ripple of laughter and the night carries on as it was.

I take my seat beside Artemis again, finishing the last of my beer. Her bow is leaned against her chair, a reminder of yet another loss.

Themis may be gone but Artemis carries her memory and the notion that justice exists side by side with forgiveness. Justice being entirely different from vengeance. I understand that now.

And they say I can't be taught.

Artemis lays her head on my shoulder and I don't think about those things anymore. I feel content. There is much to do but it's all for the morning. I take a long drink of beer and she stirs on my shoulder.

Perhaps it will be afternoon.

I smile.

This is our world again. Even if it is a new world.

It is ours to protect.

This new alliance of gods. Titan and Olympian.

Nothing can stop us now.

I am roused from the thought by the sound of footsteps from the house and a deep growl from Cerberus. In a heartbeat we are armed and facing the intruder, who holds his hands up and moves slowly.

He has an angular face, a dark tan and wears a light brown jacket and blue pants. He looks like a man who knows hard work.

I like him.

"You're in the wrong place." Aphrodite says and out of the corner of my eye I see Prometheus moving around the edge of the yard, shotgun in hand.

"I'd disagree," the man says. "You're the gods that have been making front page news all over the world, correct?"

There is silence.

"I thought as much. I've come to speak to you on behalf of the mortal world. We have certain expectations. Rules, even. Rules we must discuss."

Prometheus places the shotgun against the man's head. He doesn't flinch, his eyes just flit to the side.

"I'd rather you didn't."

"Why should we have the discussion?" I realize that I have spoken, stepping forward from the group towards this man. He looks to me, amusement in his eyes.

"You are hardly the only gods on this planet. I prefer conversation to craters, I'm hoping you do as well."

I am proven wrong yet again.

There is much to do, and it will not wait for morning.

Epilogue

"Zeus is dead."

The Smith laughed, wiping the sweat from his forehead with the back of his hand, smearing grease and grime across it in the process. He was a powerfully built man, at least eight feet tall, with thick arms and legs. He could even put a solid effort in against any one of the mythically strong Cyclopes.

He would lose but it would be a good effort.

He looked to the speaker and gave her a smile.

"Well, how do you feel?"

She sighed.

"Liberated. Can we go back now?"

The Smith turned to his work and looked it over, turning it and nodding as he determined he was pleased with it.

"Yes, we can."

He wrapped the object in rolls of soft tanned leather and handed it to her gently before the heavy footsteps of two rather large men echoed in the smithy.

"You heard?"

The larger and older of the two said it, his voice didn't quite seem to suit his form. His shaved head was peppered with scars and his long brown beard was tangled and greying. He walked with a long spear but not so much for support. In public he wore a patch over a heavily scarred and empty eye socket but around here he didn't bother.

The other was taller and broader, younger too. His beard was shorter and without any grey and his hair was long and pulled back into a warrior's braid and knot.

She nodded to them and the older held open his arms for her.

She embraced him.

"Then you will go to them?"

She smiled and nodded, trying to hide her excitement about the prospect. It had been so long. It was time to return.

"You will always be welcome in our hall, them as well."

The taller one said it, leaning down to give her a quick kiss on the cheek. She had come to them for help many years ago and they had agreed to her plan. The Olympians had been as much trouble for them as her.

"Thank you. For everything. I am eternally grateful and owe you a debt."

The older one shook his head.

"No debts. We'll settle for an alliance of the gods."

"And you will have it."

The Smith said this, stepping forward and offering a large hand that was taken enthusiastically by both men.

"I will return when she is safe," he said, placing a hand on her shoulder, "to make sure she gets to them safely."

"We will await your return, Hephaestus, you have done us well and we will not forget. Your Cyclops brothers and sisters will be safe here."

Hephaestus nodded his thanks to the taller of the two, who said it. She stepped forward again.

"Thank you for everything, all of you."

She said, with a final embrace.

"Safe travel Theia, I hope it was all worth it."

Her eyes drifted for a moment, becoming unfocused.

"Me too Odin, me too."

Two men stood over a row of bodies in military uniforms under a blazing sun, one dressed in a similar uniform and the other in loose fitting khaki pants and a light button-down shirt.

"So," the one in the uniform said, waving a hand over the soldier, "this happened."

The other nodded, taking a long drag from his cigarette before flicking it at the ground. He wanted to quit, he really did, but every time he tried something like this happened.

"Do we know who it was?"

The uniformed one nodded, rubbing his chin. Didn't feel right being in this form.

"Titans. They went after the Olympians."

"Ah."

There was a long silence.

The smoker drew another cigarette from a crumpled pack and lit it, "what do we do?"

The uniformed one watched as the bodies were carried away, thinking about their options. If it was a decided action against them then it wasn't a very good one. The Titans probably hadn't even considered the other pantheons as they stomped over the world. As angry as he was that other gods might tread on their sacred ground, was it worth a war?

"I think we talk to them, maybe it was a misunderstanding."

The smoker laughed until he coughed violently, looking at his brother incredulously.

"You've changed Osiris, where's your fire?"

The older rounded on his little brother, eyes burning bright, "watch your tongue Set, or I'll take it."

Set chuckled and put up a hand, "very intimidating. As you wish. Let us talk with these Titans then. They seem to have some power."

Osiris rubbed his jawline and smiled.

"They do seem to have power. Yes, it would be good to talk to them."

"And if they are unapologetic? If they intended the slight?"

Osiris laughed and snatched the cigarette from his brother, taking his own drag.

"Then we kill them."

Printed in Great Britain
by Amazon